SIMPLE + COMPLICATED = IMPOSSIBLE

IMPOSSIBLE

(THE BLAKE FAMILY SERIES #2)

R.C. STERN

Cover Design by StunningBookCovers.com
Formatting by Polgarus Studio

ISBN-13: 978-0-9965278-3-5 (Kindle)
ISBN-13: 978-0-9965278-4-2 (epub)
ISBN-13: 978-0-9965278-5-9 (print)
ISBN-13: 978-0-9965278-6-6 (print)

In memory of those that have been loved and lost.
Memoratus in aeternum.

CHAPTER ONE

April

CARI

A baby.

Oh. My. God.

I'm going to have a baby.

Breathe.

Don't panic.

Take a deep breath.

Oh dear God. This cannot be happening. I should have paid attention to my body. I should have noticed I had skipped my period, but with everything that has happened over the past month it slipped my mind. What if I have hurt the baby? I express my concern to the doctor that my negligence may have harmed the fetus, but she assures me I have nothing to worry about, and the sonogram will confirm everything is fine.

My mind is nothing but a blur as I leave the doctor's office. I cannot return to work in this state. I pull my phone out of my bag and call my superior. I am not ready to share my news yet so I concoct an excuse. Fortunately for me she is understanding and accepts it. As I wait for the elevator, I place a hand on my flat abdomen. It's hard to believe I have a precious life growing inside of me. I made a promise to myself a long time ago that I would never allow myself to be in the same predicament as my mother. The irony strikes me and as inappropriate as it is, I laugh. History does have a habit of repeating itself.

After making the appointment to see the obstetrician next week, I turn on the television and plop down on the couch. This should be a happy moment for me, but I feel anything but. Can I do this? Can I raise this baby by myself? My mother had her parents to help her raise me, but I'm alone and pregnant with *his* baby in another city. Just thinking about him is painful, and the tears threaten to spill. Should I tell him? What will he say? Will he want the baby? Can this baby bring us back together? *No.* I shake the ridiculous thought out of my head. He's chosen to move on with Rochelle. If I tell him, he will think I'm using the baby to get him back. A baby will only complicate his life with her, and that's the last thing he needs.

I cover my face with my hands and sob. Exhaustion eventually takes over and I fall asleep. The ringtone coming from my cell phone awakens me from my nap.

"Hello?"

"Thank God you answered. Are you okay?" It's Rodrigo sounding relieved.

I look at the time and see that it's nine o'clock. I was supposed to call Rodrigo when I got home.

"Yes, I am. I'm sorry for not calling. I fell asleep."

"Hunter, she's okay." I hear him say. "What did the doctor say? Please tell me everything is fine and that you don't have a terminal illness."

I roll my eyes. He can really be dramatic. "I don't have a terminal illness."

"Thank goodness. We have been worried. Did the doctor say why you haven't been feeling well?"

"Yes, she did." I pause for a moment and take a deep breath before continuing. "I'm pregnant."

"What?!" Rodrigo screeches causing me to pull the phone away from my ear. Gosh, he's loud.

"I'm having a baby."

"She's having a baby," he repeats to Hunter. "I thought the two of you were using protection."

"I was on the pill. The doctor told me the pill is not one hundred percent effective."

"That's why both partners are supposed to use protection."

I rub my forehead. I really am not up for a lecture right this moment.

"Are you keeping the baby?"

"Yes, of course I'm keeping the baby."

"When do you plan on telling him?"

"I'm not."

"What do you mean you're not?"

"There's no need for him to know."

"He has to know. That's his child you're carrying. How can you not tell him?"

"He's with someone else now. I'm not going to drop this bomb on him so he can think I am using the baby to get him back."

"Who cares? And that's ludicrous coming from you. Suppose he finds out?"

"How will he? I live in Boston now. He has no reason to be here."

"What if you run into him while you're back in New York?"

He has a good point. I had not given thought to that at all. I can lie about it. "I won't tell him it's his."

"What? You can only get away with it if the baby looks nothing like him. Cari, he has to know regardless if he is with someone else or not. Do you really want this baby to grow up not knowing who his or her father is like you did?"

Oh, he just had to go there. "I turned out perfectly fine," I snap back.

"I have never known you to be irrational until now. You cannot deprive him of his parental right. Besides, he needs to pay for child support."

"I can be both the mother and father to this baby. I don't need child support from him." I have a generous amount of money saved between the insurance policies and the inheritance Grams and Gramps left to me not to mention the money from the sale of their house that I can use if I need to. I do not need Deven's money.

"Aye niña. I think the pregnancy hormones are clouding your head. A baby is a huge responsibility."

"I'm not giving the baby up."

"If you have this baby, you're not going to have much of a life. Men are not going to want to go out with you if you have baggage."

"My life will revolve around my baby. The baby comes first." I can't even think about another man in my life right now or any time in the foreseeable future. "And I'm not ready for a relationship any time soon."

"Not now, but maybe later." Perhaps maybe never.

"I don't want to discuss this anymore. I'm alone, and I really need your support and Hunter's."

"Of course we'll support you."

"I'm going to lean on the both of you a lot."

"Lean all you want."

"Love you."

"Love you too. Now go take a nice relaxing bath and try to get some rest for you and the baby. We'll see you next week."

I fall back asleep dreaming of a beautiful dark haired boy with dimples and sapphire eyes exactly like his father's.

~ * ~

Rodrigo and Hunter arrive a couple of days early so they can accompany me to my first ultrasound. I lay down on the table as instructed, and Hunter and Rodrigo stand to the side.

"I can't wait to see the little squirt," Rodrigo says.

"Me too," Hunter concurs.

The door opens and a lady wearing a white lab coat walks in and closes the door behind her.

"Hello Carilyn. I'm Dr. Bryant."

She's my OB? She looks like she recently graduated from med school.

"Hello Dr. Bryant," I say.

"She's so young," I hear Hunter say to Rodrigo.

"Looks can be deceiving," Dr. Bryant says not looking or sounding offended by his comment. "And you are?"

"I'm Rodrigo, Cari's best friend. And this is my partner, Hunter."

"Very nice to meet you both."

"Likewise," Rodrigo says.

Dr. Bryant turns her attention to me. "Are you ready to see your baby?"

"I am," I reply eagerly.

She explains what she will be doing, and then asks me to roll the bottom of my shirt above my abdomen. She then squirts some warm gel over my abdomen, and rolls a probe over my belly. I focus on the black and white image on the monitor, and there it is…my precious baby.

"Where is the baby?" Rodrigo asks.

"The baby is right here," Dr. Bryant replies moving the mouse so the arrow on the monitor is pointing to the baby.

I am amazed at the picture on the monitor.

"It looks like a peanut!" Rodrigo says.

"I think it's amazing," Hunter says.

After the sonogram, she tells us to meet her in her office. Rodrigo and Hunter leave the room with her to give me time to wipe off the remaining gel on my abdomen. Together we enter her office and she gives me the sonogram pictures, a bottle of prenatal vitamins, and tells me what to expect over the next few weeks until my next appointment.

Baby and I are hungry so we hop on the "T" to Cambridge to have lunch at my favorite Thai restaurant. We're seated immediately and a waiter comes to our table shortly after to take our orders. We look at the sonogram pictures of the baby again.

"I can't believe that is inside you," Rodrigo says.

"I can hardly believe it myself. It's so tiny," I say.

"There's something we have been wanting to tell you," Hunter says to me.

I put down the pictures. "What is it?"

Rodrigo and Hunter exchange glances. What is going on between these two?

"Rodrigo asked me to marry him."

My eyes widen and my mouth opens in surprise. "Really?"

"Yes."

"That's so wonderful! Congratulations!"

"Thank you. And we want you to be our best lady."

"I'd be honored. Thank you. Have you picked a date yet?"

"That depends on you."

I don't understand. "On me?"

"You let us know when you can take off and we will pick that date to get married at City Hall."

"City Hall? What happened to a big wedding?"

"Hunter and I compromised. We will have a smaller wedding and save our money to buy a house in the suburbs instead."

"Sounds like you both have it all planned out."

"We do. And now that you're having a baby we are thinking of starting our own family too, but maybe in a year or two. Wouldn't it be great if our kids can play together?"

I smile envisioning the three of us at a playground chasing after our kids. "Yes, it would be. I never thought I'd have my own so soon."

"Neither did we, but consider it to be a blessing," Rodrigo says.

Yes, this baby is a blessing. And I'm going to give this baby so much love and more.

CHAPTER TWO

CARI

Finally beginning to feel much better and less tired, I travel to New York so I can spend the weekend with Rodrigo. This weekend trip is to celebrate my belated birthday. Unfortunately, Hunter cannot join us as his grandfather is very sick and he had to fly back to California.

It's late by the time I arrive in Manhattan so Rodrigo meets me at the parking garage. He grabs my bag and hugs me tightly.

"I've missed you," I tell him as we begin our short walk back to the apartment.

"And I've missed you. You must be exhausted."

"I am. I've had a long day."

"I know. Work, and then the drive here. Thanks for coming. I'm so happy we get a shopping weekend to ourselves." I shake my head and laugh. My best friend is very much a shopaholic.

We enter the lobby and wait for the elevator. I catch him staring at my belly.

"You don't look pregnant at all."

I press my hand to my abdomen and show off my small bump.

"Now you do."

"I'll probably start showing more in the next few weeks."

The elevator doors open and we step in for the ride up.

"You do look adorable sweetie."

"It's still surreal that I'm going to have a baby."

"Well you are, and I am so going to spoil her more than Hunter will."

"Her? How do you know I am having a girl?"

"I don't, but I am hoping it's a girl. What are you hoping for?"

I shrug. "A healthy baby is what I am hoping for. I will be happy regardless of the sex. This baby will be so loved."

"Nothing less. And Hunter and I will also shower the baby with tons of love." He unlocks the door and lets me in first. "Guess what I got?"

"What?"

"I picked up a cake from our favorite bakery."

A big smile appears on my face. "The signature cake?"

"Of course *dahling*."

"I can't wait to have a piece!"

"Then let me go cut a slice for each of us. Go sit at the table. I'll bring yours out to you."

Rodrigo comes over shortly with a slice of the red velvet crepe cake. I immediately dig in. It's so delicious, and I think baby likes it too.

"I miss this. I wish they had a shop in Boston."

"Take the rest of the cake back with you then."

"I will. Baby and I are going to enjoy every last crumb." I put another forkful of cake in my mouth. "How is Hunter's grandfather?"

Rodrigo shakes his head. "Not any better. Hunter doesn't think he has much time left. He's an emotional wreck."

I wish I could be there to comfort him. I'll make sure to send him a text later. Rodrigo and I catch up over the next hour or so before a yawn escapes me.

"You should get some sleep."

I will not argue with him on that. Being pregnant makes me quite tired. He brings my bag into my room and places it on the bed. I follow him in and sit down on my bed. "I wish I wasn't so tired so we can keep talking."

"We have plenty of time to talk tomorrow."

I give him a nod. "Good night Rodrigo."

"Good night Cari."

He leaves my room and closes the door behind him. I unpack my suitcase and open the closet door. There's a photo album on the bottom shelf. I pick it up and bring it with me to the bed. I flip through the pages of photos of

Rodrigo and I. There are pictures of us from our high school and college years. Looking at the old pictures bring back such great memories and makes me smile until I come across a photo that wipes the smile off my face. It's a picture of Deven and I at Alana's wedding. That day rushes back to me. He looked so dashing. I can see and almost feel the love he had for me. I miss his smile. I miss his arms around me, and the adoring way he used to look at me.

I lean back against the headboard and splay my hands on my swollen belly. I close my eyes wishing things were different. I allow myself to imagine his elation when I tell him we are having a baby. I envision him lifting me off the ground and spinning me around, and then drawing me in for a long kiss. The vision starts to fade, and I open my eyes to face reality again. What should be isn't, and all that I have left of him is the baby. A baby he will never know about.

~ * ~

Rodrigo has planned a day of shopping and eating. Besides being constantly tired, I am also constantly hungry. Tonight Rodrigo is taking me out for my belated birthday dinner, and he refuses to give me a hint where he is taking me. He insists on it being a surprise. I can hardly wait to see where he will take me. We started our morning shopping in Greenwich Village, and worked our way to SoHo. I do miss the shopping in New York. Boston has great shopping, but it doesn't compare to the shopping here. It's nearly noon when we come upon a chic baby boutique. We go in and I am immediately in love with all the cute clothing the store carries. I walk over to one of the racks with the pretty dresses.

"I see you're hoping for a girl too," Rodrigo says.

"This dress caught my attention and I wanted a closer look at it." I take the dress off the rack and look it over. It's yellow with a lace overlay and a white sash around the middle and really is pretty.

Rodrigo examines the dress. "I am going to spoil my godchild with only the best."

"Babies grow so quickly. I rather you invest the money instead into a savings bond or something that will have a return."

He rolls his eyes. "Hunter can do that. I want to dress the baby in style." He picks up a ceramic piggy bank off the shelf next to the rack of dresses. "This is my contribution to her savings. I'm definitely getting the baby one of these oinkers."

The piggy bank is cute. It even has a rhinestone studded pink bow on top of its head. "Alright. I'll let you get that for the baby."

"Good. And you have to have this too." He points to a white picture frame with a side panel inscribed "Love at First Sight."

I can put the sonogram picture in it. "It's absolutely perfect!"

"Yes, it is. I'm buying it for you." He grabs the frame, and then looks at the skincare section. He picks up a tube of lotion and reads the back. "You need this. It helps with stretch marks." I haven't thought about stretch marks. "I'm also buying this for you. Stretch marks are so unattractive," he says and walks up to the register to pay for it.

"It's part of being pregnant."

"Honey, you still need to look good when you're pregnant. Haven't you seen how glamorous the celebrity mommies are?"

"I'm not a celebrity."

"Dating Deven elevated you to the celebrity status."

There's a shooting pain in my heart at the mention of his name. I close my eyes and shake my head.

"I'm sorry hun. I didn't mean to bring him up."

"I know you didn't mean to. It's just...I just wish things had turned out differently."

Rodrigo hugs me. After the purchase we grab a quick lunch before finishing up our shopping. As Rodrigo and I stroll down the street I feel a tightness around my abdomen. A sharp pain forces me to stop walking. I put my hands on my hips and take a couple of deep breaths.

"What's wrong?"

Ow! There goes the pain again. The pain feels like bad cramps, and I clutch my belly.

"Maybe...it's something...I ate," I manage to say in between deep breaths.

"Let's go find a place where you can sit down." Rodrigo puts his arm around my waist to support me. The pain becomes more intense as we continue to walk down the street looking for a place to sit. Why are there no benches on the sidewalk?

"Rodrigo, I can't…" I am trying to speak in between breaths, "walk… anymore."

"Oh sweetie, you don't look so good. I need to get you home so you can rest."

Rodrigo hails a cab to take us back to the apartment. He helps me into bed letting me know he is available if I need him. I nod and fall asleep immediately. Sometime later I wake up, but something doesn't feel right. My underwear and shorts are soaked. Gosh, I must have been so tired that I pee'd on myself. I get up to remove my clothes and glance down at the sheets. Sheer terror hits me instantly. *Oh my God!* My underwear, shorts, and sheets are stained with blood. I let out a scream, and Rodrigo comes running into my room. His eyes become wide when he sees the blood.

"Holy shit Cari! You need to go to the ER now!"

The ER? I feel as if the air has been sucked out of my body. I can't bring myself to move. Rodrigo reaches for my cell phone and dials 9-1-1.

The cramps are excruciating and I clutch my abdominal area. *Oh God, please don't let anything happen to my baby. Please, please, please.* I'm frightened, and trembling. The uncontrollable tears are rolling down my face. I hear Rodrigo on the phone, but I can't make out what he's saying. Suddenly everything becomes dark.

CHAPTER THREE

CARI

I open my eyes to unfamiliar surroundings. I roll my head to the left and see Rodrigo sitting on the chair reading a book.

"Hey." My mouth feels dry.

"Niña." Rodrigo rushes to my bedside and takes my hand. "How do you feel?"

I look at him and immediately everything rushes back to me. I splay my hand over my belly. It feels empty, and tears fill my eyes. "My baby?"

Rodrigo averts his eyes from me. When he looks back at me, his eyes are glassy. He shakes his head. "I'm sorry sweetie. They couldn't save the baby."

Oh God. No! My baby. Not my baby. I cover my face and weep. *Why my baby?* Rodrigo holds me tightly as I sob uncontrollably. This is so unfair. Remorse fills me. Am I being punished for not telling Deven?

I try to get my crying under control to attempt to ask the next question.

"Where is my baby? Did they…" I can't bear to finish the sentence. The thought of the staff disposing my baby is just unbearable.

He closes his eyes and a couple of tears escape. "I had them hold the remains until you woke up. I didn't want to make the decision."

I shudder at the thought of having to bury my precious baby that was taken away from me far too soon. "I want the baby to be with Grams and Gramps, and my mother. They must be together. I want a beautiful casket for the baby, and I want something to memorialize the baby. Something pretty that I can always keep with me."

"Of course. Whatever you want. I'll help you with all the arrangements."

Whatever I want. What I want is to have my baby back, and for Deven to be here to comfort me. I lean back on my pillow and close my eyes wishing things were different.

"I should have told Deven. I should have. If only he was here right now."

"Do you want me to call him?"

I do, but what good will that do? He doesn't know about the baby. I am just about to answer Rodrigo when the door swings open and the doctor comes in. He introduces himself, and gently tells me that I lost my baby as tears pour down my face. He explains to me that I was hemorrhaging when I was brought in. My blood pressure had dropped significantly and it caused me to pass out. My body was not ready to handle the baby, and there was nothing that could have been done to save the baby. It is absolutely devastating to hear this. He reassures me that I will be able to bear children again, but the thought of having another baby is unthinkable at this time. Before the doctor leaves, he informs me as long as my blood pressure does not drop, and there are no complications he will discharge me tomorrow.

"Do you think losing the baby is my punishment for not telling Deven?"

"Absolutely not. You heard what the doctor said." I want to believe it, but I can't escape the feeling of being punished. Rodrigo lets out a deep sigh and pats my hand. "It doesn't matter now. All that matters is you. You need to heal."

Nothing can heal the emptiness and pain in me.

~ * ~

DEVEN

The golden sun is getting ready to set. The sky is a beautiful palette of pink, blue, and white. The ocean waves gently sweep over the sand. There's a light cool breeze as we sit on the shore watching the sunset. She leans back against my chest and I pull her closer to me enfolding her in my arms.

"I wish this weekend didn't have to end."

I wish it didn't have to either. I place a kiss on the top of her head. "We can celebrate your birthday by coming back Memorial Day weekend."

She turns her head back and smiles. "I would love that." She gives me a chaste kiss, but I catch the bottom of her lip between my teeth and nibble on it. I love the taste of her. She reaches behind me and pulls my head down to her neck. Damn, I love when she does that. I gently push her down on the sand and hover over her. The wind blows a few strands across her face. I push back those strands behind her ear, and look deep into her beautiful jade eyes.

"I love you Carilyn." And I always will. She's changed my life and fills me completely. I want her to be mine forever. The ring is tucked away safely at home, and I look forward to the day she agrees to be Mrs. Deven Blake.

"I love you too."

I stroke her cheek with my thumb and lean down to kiss her.

The alarm goes off and interrupts my dream. I reach over to shut it off and roll onto my back. I run my hands up and down my face, and stare at the ceiling. That dream wasn't just a dream. It was real. Our weekend away at Kiawah Island was real and ever so vivid in my head. It was the perfect weekend. Everything had been so perfect between us then. I loved her so much. Fuck. Who am I kidding? I still love her. It's been nearly three months and my heart has not stopped aching for her each day that passes by. Brad is right. I'm not over her, and I don't know if I ever will be. But the damage to our relationship is irreparable, and we've gone our separate ways. At least she has by moving to Boston.

I slowly drag myself out of bed and put on my gym clothes. I brush my teeth, and run my fingers through my long hair to comb it. I forgo shaving and head to the hotel's fitness center where I plan to spend the next hour working out before my morning meeting at nine.

My early workout is cut short when the girl on the treadmill can't take her eyes off of me nor stop talking to me. It's a feeble attempt to pick me up. She is a pretty thing, but I'm not interested in her. Back in my suite, I strip out of my sweaty gym clothes and head into the bathroom for a shower. After my shower, I order breakfast off of the In-Room Dining menu. I reach into the closet and pull out a light blue shirt and black pants to put on. While I wait for my breakfast to be brought up to my room, I power on my MacBook. I still have an hour before my online meeting begins with Brayden, my VP of Development and Construction; Adam, my Development Project Manager;

and Brad. I open my files and search for the CPM on Seattle. I quickly go through it once more and make additional notes. My breakfast finally arrives as I begin to check my emails.

The meeting begins promptly at nine. I start it off by going over all the notes I made on the CPM. In the middle of the video conference, I gaze out the window at the sheets of rain coming down in Seattle while Brayden and Adam give me an update on the progress of BG's new environmentally friendly office building. This building is the first of its kind in my company. If Dad was still alive to see this construction taking place he would no doubt be impressed.

I have been working relentlessly the past couple of months to move things ahead in the company. It's helped me to keep my mind off of Cari. With the west coast projects progressing it's time to focus on Hong Kong and decide who I will send there to take on that project.

Being in Seattle seems to be working out much better for me. I will remain in Seattle over the next few weeks before going back to New York for May's graduation. Last week while I was in Los Angeles, Rochelle persistently called me. She's hoping to have another chance with me, but it's something I cannot give her. I have to make this clear to her soon so she stops wasting time pining over me. First, I have to speak to Kait and get her situation taken care of before I break the news to Rochelle.

"Deven, do you have any other matters to discuss?" Brad asks.

"No," I say as I shake my head.

"Okay, then. Looks like we're all done. Have a good day gentlemen."

I log off the meeting. My cell phone rings and the caller ID shows Brad's number.

"What's up?"

"When are you leaving Seattle to come back?"

"On my birthday."

"Now that definitely calls for a celebration."

"Not feeling it this year." I have no desire to celebrate my birthday. The one person I want to spend it with is in another city, and she has moved on with her life. What if she met someone else? Jealousy sears through me at that thought. She should be with me.

"You need a night out."

The last time I caved into his request for a night out was the night I met Cari. I close my eyes as I remember that night when she caught my eye. Beautiful and shy. I fell in love with her then and there. I used to think love at first sight was bullshit until I saw her. She was there to celebrate her birthday. *Her birthday.* Before we broke up I had plans to take her back to Kiawah Island for her birthday. We were supposed to celebrate it together, and then when we returned to New York I was going to ask her to marry me. *Fuck. Enough of this. It's over.*

"I guess I do."

"You do. It'll be fun. We're going to have a good time."

A good time. He better be right.

CHAPTER FOUR

June

CARI

I had been inconsolable at the hospital when I finally got to hold my baby. The baby was so small it fit in the palm of my hand. Oh God, it was the most precious thing I had ever held. I couldn't take my eyes off of my baby. It had a head, arms, legs, tiny fingers, and toes. So perfect.

The days following my discharge seem to be fuzzy. The only thing I remember is selecting a casket for the baby. It was one of the most difficult things I had ever done. How does a parent survive the loss of a child? No parent should have to experience such devastation.

Dark clouds loom in the gray skies and there's a loud clap of thunder as Hunter, Rodrigo, the priest, and I stand in the cemetery. Hunter had returned early from California to be here for the burial. The three of us circle the baby's casket as the priest leads us through prayers and blessings. Once the priest finishes, Hunter and Rodrigo reach down to grab the straps underneath the casket. I stare at the tiny white casket as the two of them slowly and steadily lower it into the ground. The priest comes over to me and says something, but I am not listening to what he's telling me. The pain of losing my child is agonizing. Rodrigo puts his arm around my shoulder and Hunter takes my hand, and together we walk to the car.

I spent two more days in New York before coming home to Boston. I drop my bag in the living room and go into the kitchen for a bottle of water. The picture of my baby from the sonongram visit hangs on the refrigerator door. Tears fill my eyes. I pull down the picture and hold it close to my heart as big fat tears roll down my cheeks. This picture is all that I have left of the baby.

Did my baby know how much I loved him or her? The pain in my heart is excruciating. It hurts like hell. I wanted the baby so much.

I think of Deven. How I wish he was here to hold me, and to comfort me. I need him so much. How do people move on when they lose their baby? How do they pick up all the shattered pieces of their heart and continue living each day? Will I ever get over this lugubrious feeling? I wish I could just close my eyes and never wake up again so I don't have to keep hurting and feeling empty.

Monday rolls around and somehow I manage to make it through my first day back at work. When I reach home there is a package in front of my door. One of my neighbor's must have brought it in from the outside and left it here for me. I look at the shipper's address. It's the baby's memorial keepsake. I open the door and bring the package inside. I place my purse on the table, and rip open the box. I remove the item from the box and stare at the stacked three tiered pyramid wooden block set monogrammed with the baby's name and birth date. It's beautiful and perfect. I bring it into the living room and place it on the bookshelf right next to the ultrasound picture.

~ * ~

DEVEN

I exit the terminal rolling my suitcase behind me. I see Mauricio waiting for me.

"Mauricio, good to see you."

"Welcome back sir. It's good to see you too, and happy birthday."

"Thank you."

"Only the one suitcase?"

"Yes, that's all I brought with me."

"Traveling lightly?" He takes the suitcase from me and rolls it behind him.

"Indeed I am."

"It's good to have you back sir."

"Yeah. It's good to be back." I pat him on the shoulder.

He opens the car door for me and I slide in. He shuts the door and places my suitcase in the trunk. I sit back and close my eyes as Mauricio drives away from the airport. It's my birthday, and I have been flooded with birthday wishes, but it feels anything but happy.

My penthouse is immaculate as it should be. It's been weeks since I have been home, but my housekeeper has been tending to it each week. I pull the suitcase into the hallway and leave it outside of the master suite. Since the breakup with Cari, I have not slept in this room. The bed feels too empty without her in it.

I turn around and head into my home office to start working. While my laptop is powering up I lean back in my chair. I have always been confident about everything I do. When I see something I want, I go after it. I don't let anything good pass me by. Except for Cari.

As much as I try to move on without her, I find it impossible to do so. I fucking miss her. I always wonder how she is and what she's doing. Is she happy? Is she okay? She absorbs my thoughts day and night. Night and day. Does she think of me as often as I think of her? Does she even think of me at all?

How I quickly revert back to working longer hours now that I'm not with her. It's the only thing I look forward to. I have no desire to go on any dates. None whatsoever. Cari ruined me. No one will ever compare to her. My phone rings and disrupts me from my thoughts. It's Brad calling.

"Hey."

"Happy birthday man! Welcome back."

"Thanks. How's everything in the office?"

"Everything is running smooth. I got it all under control. I wanted to find out when you wanted to meet up."

"Can you get here for six?"

"Yep. I'll leave here in about forty-five minutes or so and give you a call when I'm on my way up there."

"Sounds good."

I arrive ten minutes early to the bar. I take a seat and order a beer. A beer? I seldom order a beer. What the hell is going on with me?

"Hello there. Drinking alone?" A brunette pulls out the barstool and sits next to me. Here it goes again. Another one trying to pick me up.

"Not for long."

She flashes a seductive smile, and moves a little closer to me.

"I'm meeting someone here."

"Oh," she says sounding disappointed. "I was hoping you would buy me one, but it shouldn't come as a surprise an attractive guy like you wouldn't be here alone."

Before Cari, I would have bought this girl a drink, and then end up back at her place. But the moment I laid eyes on Cari I was a goner. She had a hold on me then, and she will always have a hold on me.

"You're an attractive lady, but I'm not interested at all." She pouts, but I'm not falling for it. I'm done with women like her.

"Hey D."

Brad's timing is impeccable.

"Hey."

We give each other a man hug.

"Order your drink and meet me at the table over there." I point to the table in the far back corner.

"Sure thing."

I grab my drink and walk over to the table without saying another word to the brunette. I sit down at the table and check my emails on my phone as I wait for Brad to join me. After I am done checking my emails I turn around to see what is taking him so long. Oh fuck. The brunette has made her move on him. I agreed to come out tonight and I'll be damned if I am going to celebrate alone. I get up and head back to the bar to pull him away.

CHAPTER FIVE

CARI

Trying to get through the past few weeks have been difficult. Each day had developed into a pattern of crying myself to sleep and waking up with a heavy heart and tears in my eyes. There was no desire to do anything except mourn the baby Deven and I had created. Hunter and Rodrigo have come to be with me every weekend to help me move past this insisting that my unborn child will always be with me, and that life does go on.

Last Saturday, Rodrigo dragged me out for a day of beauty. The first stop was to the hair salon. He and the stylist discussed different hairstyles and which one would be the most flattering on me. After the stylist worked his magic with the scissors on my hair, I could hardly believe the transformation. My long hair had been cut to my shoulders with different layers giving my limp and dull hair much needed texture and volume. I had to admit I looked incredible with the new haircut. Pleased with the results, Rodrigo pulled me along to our spa treatment afterwards. We both had a one hour aromatherapy session, and then much needed manicures and pedicures. At the end of the day I felt like a whole new person. Rodrigo and Hunter were both right. *I am still alive.* I need to start living again…if not for me, for the sake of my baby.

It's Friday night and a bunch of us from work gather at the bar down the street to celebrate Faith's birthday. A round of tequila was ordered and we raise our shot glasses to Faith wishing her a happy birthday before downing it. Another round is ordered, but I opt out of it. One shot is good enough for me.

"Cari, I think someone is checking you out," Faith says leaning into me. I turn around to see who she is looking at and notice the cute guy three booths away staring at me. *Oh!* I blush and turn back to Faith.

"He's cute."

"Cute? I think you better get your eyes checked. He is h-o-t," she whispers to me so her boyfriend does not hear her.

Hot. That's the word I would use to describe Deven. Oh God, what am I doing? I should not compare this guy to Deven. The waitress comes over to me and points to the cute guy who is still watching me. She passes along the message that he wants to buy me a drink. He's smiling at me and I surprise myself by giving him a shy smile in return.

"Really?" I ask the waitress and she nods. "Okay. Umm, I'll have an appletini please."

"You got it. Be right back with it."

Faith leans into me again. "He wants to buy you a drink? Definitely wants to get to know you."

Know me or hopes to get lucky tonight? If it's the second choice, forget it. I'm not that kind of girl. I am just about to say this to Faith when she interrupts me and tells me in her squeaky voice that he is coming towards me. My eyes widen. Faith motions for me to turn around and meet him. I do so and seeing him up close makes my heart beat faster. He is pretty hot, but not as hot as Deven. Oh no! I did it again. It's not fair to compare anyone to Deven.

"Hello," he says first.

"Hi."

As if on cue, the waitress returns with my drink.

"Thanks for the drink," I say and take a sip of it. He winks at me and I feel my cheeks heat up.

"You're welcome. I'm Grady." He offers a handshake.

"Hi Grady," I say as I shake his hand. He has a firm grip. "It's nice to meet you. I'm Cari."

"Nice to meet you as well Cari. You're here with your friends?"

"Friends and co-workers. One of them has a birthday and we came here to celebrate her special day."

"Happy birthday to her then."

I look back to see if I could introduce him to Faith, but she looks like she is quite wrapped up in conversation so I point her out to him instead. "Are you here with your co-workers too?"

He rubs his chin. "Yeah. Where do you work?"

"Over at the POSH hotel. What about you?"

"At McFarlane's Investments."

"Where is that located?"

"It's about five blocks from where you work."

"That's not far."

"Not at all. Do you come here often?"

"Not really. I recently moved back to the area a few months ago." I take another sip of my delicious appletini. I am not normally chatty, but I did have two drinks earlier and this appletini is number three. Maybe this should be my last drink.

"Where did you move from?"

"New York."

"New York, huh? Well, Boston's much better."

I shrug. "They're almost the same to me."

We talk for some time mostly about things to do in Massachusetts. Then he asks if he can take me out to dinner tomorrow night. I'm hesitant to say yes. Am I ready to hit the dating scene again? Deven wasted no time in running back to Rochelle. *I need to move on.* Surely I can do this. It's only dinner. Nothing more. I agree to it and we exchange phone numbers before rejoining the group of people we are with.

The gang decides to call it a night after another hour. Faith had too much to drink and can barely stand on her own. Her boyfriend carries her out to his car to take her home. I am most certain I will hear from her tomorrow. She will want me to recap every detail of my conversation with Grady.

As I had predicted, Faith calls me in the morning wanting to know everything that happened between Grady and I. I tell her and she is excited for me. I can't help feeling a bit excited as well. I call Rodrigo after speaking with her and tell him about Grady. He has been encouraging me to start dating again and is ecstatic to hear that I am making an attempt to do so. I can't rush this, and just need to take this one step at a time.

~ * ~

Grady picks me up and takes me to an Indian restaurant in Cambridge. During dinner, I learn that this ruggedly handsome man grew up in Maine and is the youngest of four boys. He also attended Boston University, and graduated two years before I did. He currently lives in Cambridge which explains his knowledge of the area.

"What made you move from New York City to Boston?"

I take a deep breath. I do not want to divulge the real reason why I left Manhattan so I stick to the story I have been telling those who have asked. "I needed a change."

"Ah, I see. And could that change have had anything to do with a boyfriend?"

My God, he's perceptive. I shrug. "It's something I prefer not to speak about."

"That's perfectly fine. Whatever the reason may be I'm glad for it because it brought us together."

Change. Maybe he's the change I need. He pays for dinner and we leave the restaurant. Once we're outside, he takes my hand and holds it. There is no spark between us like there was when Deven and I had first touched. I'm not sure if I am ready to let a guy hold my hand, but a little voice in my head keeps reminding me to take another small step ahead and allow Grady to hold my hand. He must have sensed my discomfort and immediately releases my hand.

"I'm sorry. I should have asked. I wasn't sure." He places one hand behind his neck looking uncomfortable.

"No, it's quite okay. I was just a bit surprised." I force myself to take his hand back. I have to move on. I can do this.

His eyes travel down to our hands and then back up at me. "Want to get some ice cream?"

"Ice cream sounds good."

"There's this ice cream shop that serves the classic flavors, but also has some unique flavors."

"Unique flavors such as?"

"Such as sweet potato, and avocado." It sounds unappealing.

"Have you tried any of those flavors?"

"I've had the avocado one."

"How was it?"

He makes a face. "Thank God it was just a sample."

I laugh. I haven't laughed in such a long time that it feels good to start to feel other emotions once again.

On our way to the ice cream shop, Grady recalls fond childhood memories of his father taking him and his siblings to the local ice cream shop during the summer months. There are some very interesting flavors on the menu, but I stick with plain and simple vanilla. He orders a flavor that supposedly tastes like clam chowder and offers me a taste. The smell of it makes me shake my head. *Gross!* How he can stand the smell of it as he takes a bite of the ice cream? He gets ice cream on his nose and it makes me giggle. I reach for a napkin and wipe it off for him. I overhear an older couple in line mentioning how cute we are together. Such a comment should make me feel flattered, but I don't feel that way. Grady is attractive and very much a gentleman, but this is only our first date. It's too soon to consider us a couple.

Grady walks me back to my apartment after we finish our ice cream, but I don't invite him in. It's way too early to do such a thing.

"Hey, thanks so much for tonight."

"You're welcome. If you're free during the week maybe we can do something after work."

"Certainly."

"Great." He holds my gaze and I wonder if he is thinking about kissing me. He scratches the back of his head instead. "I guess I should head back home. Have a good night Cari."

"You too."

I watch him leave before going inside. I take out my phone and call Rodrigo. He picks up on the first ring.

"It's about time I heard from you. So how did it go?"

"I had a nice time tonight."

"Good. I'm so glad to hear it. Did he try anything with you?"

"No. He was a complete gentleman." I describe my date night to Rodrigo.

"He is a true gentleman."

"He wants to take me out again."

"Are you going to tell him yes?"

"I don't know."

"Why not?"

I toy with a loose thread on one of my toss pillows. "He's really nice, but throughout the entire night I kept thinking of Deven."

"Seriously?"

"I tried not to."

"You need to forget about him. He most definitely isn't spending time thinking about you. I get that you fell in love with him, but people can also fall out of love. People of his status usually end up with people who are of the same status. You no longer have any ties to him. Forget him." Rodrigo is right. "You are going to get past this, and one day you will find someone better than Deven. Maybe Grady is that someone better." Can Grady be that person? "But you will never know if you don't let go of Deven."

But how do I do that? How do I let go of him?

CHAPTER SIX

DEVEN

The commencement ceremony is taking place on the school's football field. I wish Dad was still alive so he could watch with much pride as May graduates. He would be so proud of her and her achievements. Mom, Brad, and I arrive early and seat ourselves in the front row. The parents of May's friends stop to talk to Mom and I. I catch the mothers looking at me and turn away. No sense in giving them the wrong idea.

The ceremony was short, and we watched proudly as she was called up and awarded her diploma. After the ceremony, we wait for May in the back parking lot. I step aside and send her a text letting her know where we are. I join Mom and Brad again as they talk to some of the other parents.

"Deven. How have you been?" I turn and see Miles. He is the father of May's best friend, and a successful investment banker who always wants to know about the new development projects my company is taking on. I haven't seen him since the funeral.

"I'm good Miles. And how have you been?"

"Can't complain."

He starts engaging me in a conversation about commercial real estate. I need to get the fuck away from him. He always wants to be in my business instead of minding his own. Brad's mind reading talent comes in handy and he interrupts Miles claiming he needs to urgently speak to me. *Thank God*. I excuse myself and follow Brad. When we are further away from Miles I begin to search for May.

"Mayleen has grown to be one fine lady."

I narrow my eyes at him. "Hey, that's my sister you're talking about."

"I'm sorry man. No disrespect, but she is beautiful. She's going to have tons of guys hanging around her constantly at college."

"Like she does now?"

If I'm not mistaken, I think I just saw Brad's jaw tighten.

"She has a lot of guys around her now?"

"Thought you knew that."

"She's not my sister. How would I know such a thing?"

"You've been like a brother to her. Thought she would have mentioned it."

"Hi Deven." I turn around to see a group of May's friends checking me out.

"Ladies," I respond. *Go find boys your age.* "Congratulations to all of you." There's a chorus of thank you's from them. One of them waves at me, but I ignore her. Way too young and definitely not my type.

I finally find May and give her some time to say good-bye to her friends. When she has finally finished her adieus, we go to dinner. May's best friend and her family join us. Brad is sandwiched between May and her best friend leaving me to sit next to Miles who bores me to death as he talks endlessly about mindless shit. Why couldn't he have sat next to Brad and talked about investment futures instead?

~ * ~

I'm up at the crack of dawn and head into the office early. It's going to feel good to be back in my office. I haven't stepped foot into my office since my father's funeral. I walk in expecting to find a mass of files sitting on my desk, but to my surprise there are only a few files lying on my desk. Leave it to my efficient assistant to keep me organized. She's unquestionably on the top of my list for a salary increase.

I sit behind my desk, put on my glasses and start going through the files. I pull out the file for the next property we are looking to acquire in Miami.

"So you're finally back?"

I look up to find Alana standing by the door to my office.

"Hello, Alana. Good to see you too."

"When did you get back?"

"Wednesday. May graduated on Friday."

"Congratulations to her."

"Thank you."

"Which college did she decide on?"

"Unfortunately she chose Princeton." I am not at all happy that she did not choose my alma mater.

"What do you have against Princeton?"

Alana definitely does not know much about prestigious schools. My school is by far much better than Princeton.

"Everything. Now what brings you to my office?"

"Nothing. I came over to drop something off at Cat's desk and saw your door was opened."

Right. Note to self, always shut the damn door behind me.

"How long are you back for this time?"

I shrug. "Probably another week or two, and then I'm back out to the west coast to monitor the progress. Hong Kong is moving along. There's going to be less staff here over the next couple of months as I temporarily relocate some of them to Hong Kong."

"For how long?"

"At least a year."

"You're really stretching this office thin. Hire the locals in Hong Kong instead."

"We'll manage here." And we will. If not, I will see to it that we hire replacements or shift people around if we have to.

"I spoke to Cari."

Just hearing her name makes my heart pump harder. "Oh yeah?"

"Yeah."

"How is she?" I ask trying to sound nonchalant.

"She's better now."

What does she mean by that? "Better? What do you mean? Was she ill?"

"She was."

What was wrong with her? I want to ask Alana, but decide against it. She'll tell me on her own will.

"I'm glad she's feeling better then."

She stands there with her arms crossed waiting to see if I am going to ask why Cari was sick. I don't ask, and as I expected she tells me.

"She had a bad case of the flu. She lost a lot of weight because she couldn't keep anything down." The thought of Cari starving sickens me. "It's a good thing she recovered otherwise she wouldn't have met that guy."

Her words pierce through my heart like a knife. What guy? She's fucking seeing someone? I didn't think she would date again so soon. I was beginning to think I had misjudged the situation between her and her British neighbor, but now I'm not so sure. *Act cool Blake.* I pretend to be unaffected by the news.

"Well then, I hope she's happy with that British fellow."

Alana looks at me with raised eyebrows. "I'm not sure where you're getting your information from, but he's not British at all."

She's not with Mr. Britain? Shit. Who is she with then? "Doesn't matter what he is. She is free to see whomever she wants."

"It doesn't bother you at all then?"

She's getting on my nerves and I need to put an end to this conversation.

"Why should it? What she does is no longer my concern."

"You no longer care?"

"Alright Dr. Phil, you need to get going. I have a conference call I need to get on." I walk her to the door as annoyance displays on her face.

"I'll let you get to it then. See ya later."

"Yes," I say and close the door.

I lean against the door and let out the breath I had been holding in. There's a deep aching pain in me. It fucking hurts like hell to know that she is seeing someone. What a God damn fool I am to have let her go, and now it's too late.

CHAPTER SEVEN

July

DEVEN

Leigh wanted to take some time to travel, but May did not want to accompany her. May wanted to enjoy her time at home with her friends before she headed off to college. Leigh was hesitant to leave May alone for a lengthy period of time, but I strongly encouraged Leigh to go on the trip and to bring along a friend instead. She booked the trip, and she and her friend embarked on a three week tour through Europe.

While she is away, I agree to come by the house and check in on May. I pull up to the courtyard and see Brad's car. What is he doing here? I set out to look for them on the first floor passing through the empty kitchen. They're probably watching television in the basement. I head downstairs, but it's quiet.

"May? Brad?" No answer. Odd. I go back up and check to see if maybe they are upstairs in her room watching television. I can hear music through her closed bedroom door. I knock once and wait for her to let me in, but I don't hear her response. I reach for the doorknob and open the door only to see something I did not want to see.

"What is going on here?"

"Oh my God! Shit!" May screams and sinks lower under the covers as Brad rolls off of her.

"What the fuck Brad? That's my baby sister!" This can't be happening. My best friend is banging my sister? Fury is running through my veins, and I want to punch the shit out of him. "I want you both dressed and downstairs in the kitchen!" I demand. *Un-fucking-real.*

31

I am seething as I pace back and forth in the kitchen trying to make sense of this. *How did this happen? When did this start? Why did it start?* The two of them finally show up and I have them each take a seat at the island.

"Dev-"

I hold up my hand to stop him from speaking first.

"Brad, you have always been like a brother to me. What the fuck are you doing screwing my baby sister?" I run my hand through my hair.

Brad's face is filled with shame. "I'm sorry. I need to –"

May cuts him off. "I have liked Brad since I hit puberty. And he likes me. He didn't force himself on me."

"May, do you know how much older he is than you?"

"What does age have to do with anything? I like him and he likes me!"

"You're still too young for him."

"I was the one who came onto him."

She can't be serious. Is she trying to give me a coronary?

"Are you shitting me?"

She crosses her arms and looks at me rebelliously. "No, I'm not."

Brad interrupts. "I'm sorry Deven, but I have to let you know that I really care about May. She's not another notch on my bedpost."

Am I supposed to feel better hearing that come from his mouth? "Caring and sleeping with her are two different things. I can't deal with you right now Brad. I want you to get the fuck out of my house before I kill you."

He nods. Our friendship is so fucking damaged right now. I thought I could trust him. What kind of friend is he if he's sneaking around behind my back and sleeping with my sister?

"Who do you think you are? He has the right to stay here. This is my house too!" May screams at me. He turns to May and puts his hand on her arm.

"Get your hand off of her." He quickly drops his hand. "I want you to leave now before I do something I *will* regret." He quickly turns and leaves.

"You're an asshole," May says to me as she starts to run after Brad. I pull on her arm to stop her.

"How long has this been going on between the two of you?"

"Only recently after I graduated. What's the big deal?" She tries to wrestle out of my grip, but she's not strong enough.

"He's ten years older than you. You should be with someone your own age."

"I'm an adult. The guys my age are immature, and I am not in the slightest bit interested in them. I've had a thing for Brad for a long time."

"I know Brad better than you do. He's a player. If you think he's going to be your boyfriend, it's not going to happen."

"You don't know that. Sometimes it takes one person to make you change."

"Well, he's not that *one* person." She is so fucking blinded by Brad she refuses to see that he will hurt her.

"Oh? And you're an expert on relationships? When you were with Cari, you were the happiest I had ever seen you. As soon as you let her go, you fell right back to your old self. Miserable and always working like there is nothing else in life to do."

"I have an empire to run, and don't bring Cari into this."

"Why shouldn't I when you are making me as miserable as you are? Is that what you want me to be? Miserable like you? Just because you fucked up your relationship with Cari doesn't give you a right to fuck up mine."

Her comment leaves me boiling with anger. "I did not fuck anything up! She did. She was the one in the arms of another man."

May puts a hand on her hip and points at me with her free hand. "I refuse to believe she was cheating on you. She's not like that, and you will never find someone as spectacular as she is. I think you completely misinterpreted the situation, and your fucking ego won't allow you to admit it. Maybe if you didn't act like a jealous asshole and think about it you will see that she did nothing wrong. Then you would be with her right now happy and all."

"What happened between Cari and I is not your business." I never intended to tell May about what happened, but it had accidentally slipped out one night. "I'm done with talking about her."

She waves a dismissive hand. "Fine. Go on and keep being miserable, but don't take your misery out on me. I am capable of deciding who I should and should not see. I don't need your approval." She storms away.

I run my hands up and down my face in frustration. Yes, I have been miserable, but I was not taking it out on Mayleen. I only want to protect her from having her heart broken. Is that so wrong? Instead, she's pissed at me.

I reach for my keys and walk out of the house.

~ * ~

I pour myself some scotch and sit on the couch. Once upon a time everything in my world was perfect. I had my girl, my Dad was still alive, and my sister and best friend were *only* friends. How the fuck did everything spiral down so quickly? I swallow the last bit of my drink and leave the glass on the table. I lean back and reflect back to the day Dad brought May home.

"Deven, come meet your baby sister."

Ewww! Baby sister. I don't want a baby in the house. I am happy being the only child. Daddy spoils me. Now I have to share my Daddy with a baby who probably does nothing but cry and poop. Daddy pats his hand on the couch for me to sit next to him. I take a seat beside him. The moment I get a peek of her I find myself amazed at how tiny she is. She is kind of cute, and she isn't screaming.

"Do you want to hold her?" Dad asks me.

"Is she going to poop?"

Dad laughs. "I don't think so."

"Okay. I want to hold her."

"Sit back then and hold out your arms." I do as he asks, and he sets a pillow under my right arm and gently places my baby sister in it. She makes a little noise and turns her head to the right and then to the left, and smiles in her sleep. Wow.

"You're a big brother now. You will have to take care of her too."

I did not do a good job taking care of her. How could I have missed the signs? When did Brad start looking at my sister in *that* way? I have been too busy drowning in my own fucking misery to take notice. I am looking forward to the day May goes off to college. Once she is far away from Brad I hope the separation will make them both realize that they do not belong together.

CHAPTER EIGHT

CARI

Things with Grady are moving at a snail's pace. We've been seeing each other the past month, but I haven't allowed anything more to happen other than a kiss on the cheek. I still have not invited him into my apartment. He's been so patient with me, but I'm just not ready yet to take the next step.

The past couple of Sunday mornings we have spent at the gym working out together. I have been running on the treadmill for almost a half hour when my phone lights up. I'm surprised to see Mayleen's number pop up. Why is she calling me? I press the pause button on the treadmill and pick up the phone.

"Hello?"

"Hi Cari." She's sniffling. Oh my God, is she crying? Did something happen to Deven? The fear grips my heart.

"Hi Mayleen. Are you okay?"

"No. Deven…" Her voice breaks at his name, and my heart starts to beat rapidly. *Please don't let anything have happened to Deven.*

"What about Deven? Did something happen?"

"I hate him."

I let out a breath of relief. "Why? What did he do?"

"He caught Brad and I together."

Her and Brad? Together? I'm speechless.

"Cari? Are you still there?"

"Yes. You and Brad are together? As in a couple?"

"Yes. We've been together since I graduated."

Oh my. This is a recipe for disaster. Deven always hoped his sister would get over her crush for Brad.

"How did this happen between you and Brad?"

"When Deven went back to Seattle, he had Brad come over to check on Mom and I. Ever since Dad's been gone, he's been so overbearingly protective. Mom had to leave for a doctor's appointment, and I went to go shower. I headed straight to the laundry room after my shower to drop my clothes in the washer. The house was so quiet I thought Brad had left. As I was putting my laundry in the washer I noticed from the corner of my eye that Brad was standing in the doorway. He just kept staring at me. It was like an intense stare you know?"

I really don't think I want to know.

She continues on. "I added the detergent to the machine and then my towel accidentally came off."

What? "Accidentally?"

"Yeah. That wasn't supposed to happen, but I swear he couldn't take his eyes off of me so I decided to leave the towel on the floor." Mayleen starts to giggle. How can she find this funny? Just a couple of minutes ago she was crying. "I asked him if he ever saw a naked girl before." She is laughing, but I don't find any humor in this at all. "He told me I was beautiful and then I kissed him. It was totally awesome! Kissing him is so different than kissing boys my age."

Of course it is. Brad is almost ten years her senior. What were they thinking?

"Is this when Deven caught the both of you?"

"Oh no. He walked in on us having sex."

My hand instantly covers my mouth. How could they do that to Deven?

"Mayleen, do you realize you are playing with fire here?"

"There is no fire. He's into me as much as I am into him."

"This relationship you have with Brad is going to destroy his friendship with your brother."

"I won't let that happen."

"How? How can you prevent that when you just told me you did it with him?"

"I will give my brother an ultimatum."

"You cannot do that. You need to keep your distance from Brad."

"I can't, and I won't."

Oh, she is just asking for more trouble.

"Mayleen, please listen to me. Don't ruin the friendship they have. Do you think your brother deserves to lose two more people in his life?"

She doesn't respond right away.

"I'm not trying to ruin their friendship. I want to be happy and Brad makes me happy. Just because Deven's miserable doesn't mean I need to be too."

Hearing that Deven is miserable makes me feel sad for him. Is he miserable because of me, or because of Rochelle? Maybe it's something else altogether? I want to ask her, but decide it's best not to. Deven has made his choice.

"You deserve to be happy." I repeat the same words that were once told to me.

"You're right about that. And Brad makes me happy. I don't know why Deven doesn't see that."

"He's caught in the middle. You're his sister, and Brad's his best friend. It's not fair to him to have to choose even though he has to."

She is silent and I know she is giving some thought to what I just said. "I guess you're right. But what if he is the one for me?"

"You still have plenty of time to figure out if he is the one for you."

"Didn't you know that my brother was the one for you?" Hearing her ask that makes my heart ache. "Oh shit. I'm sorry Cari. I should not have asked that."

I did think Deven was the one for me, and look how that turned out. I manage to swallow the sob that threatened to come out.

"Cari?"

"Yes?"

"Do you still have feelings for Deven?"

"I fell hard and fast for him. My feelings for him are not going to disappear that quickly, but he's made his choice."

"I'm sorry Cari."

"You have nothing to be sorry for."

"Do you hate him?"

If only I could. It would be so much easier to hate him. "No, I don't hate him. I will always care about him."

"Hey baby." I feel a hand on the small of my back causing me to turn around. It's Grady. Did he hear what I just told Mayleen?

"Listen. I have to go. We'll talk again soon, okay?"

"Okay. Bye Cari."

"Bye May."

I hit the end button.

"Everything okay?" Grady asks.

I look up at him and force a smile. "Yeah."

"Are you done and ready to go?"

I give him a nod and we head to the lockers to change, but I can't stop thinking about Deven and how he must be feeling.

CHAPTER NINE

DEVEN

I read through the Miami report as I wait for Myra to show up for our meeting. I have no idea why she wants to meet with me. Perhaps she's finally resigning? Nah. She will never leave. My intercom rings and Catrina announces Myra's arrival. Three o'clock. Punctual as usual with her.

"Deven," she says as she enters my office.

"What can I do for you today Myra?"

She takes a seat, crosses her legs, and looks me square in the eyes. "I do not like my assistant."

I lean back in my chair. Since Cari's departure, she has gone through three assistants in a matter of a month. Kudos to her. It's a new company record.

"What's the problem now?"

"This one does not follow directions and turned in a proposal full of errors. I don't know how she came up with her figures."

Myra's assistants are quite careless with their work, but Myra is also at fault. She should show them how to do their work correctly. "Then teach her or get another assistant."

"You have me flying between here and L.A. I don't have the time to teach."

"What would you like me to do?" I hope she doesn't plan on asking me to teach them.

"I want you to bring Carilyn Snow back here."

WTF? She wants Cari back here? Like that's going to happen.

"I thought you had issues with her as well."

She shrugs. "I have high expectations, and she just about met all of them."

Myra is actually admitting that Cari was a good assistant. Holy shit. She never praises anyone. I knew all along how very capable Cari was. Her work was always accurate and anything assigned to her was always completed in a timely manner. Cari had potential to move up in this company, and I was in the process of trying to create a new position which would have been a promotion for her when things came to an end between us.

"It's too late Myra."

"Well, we need to find someone like her because I can no longer deal with the current one I have."

She never comes to me when she has an issue with her assistant. Why now? "Do what you have to do Myra."

"As long as I have your approval."

"You do."

"Good." She stands up. She gives me a nod and looks at me. "One more thing Deven."

"Yes, Myra?"

"It's none of my business, but Cari was good for you. You were different when you were with her."

What the hell is going with the people here? First Alana, and now Myra? "You know what Myra?"

"What?"

"You're right. It *is* none of your business. Have a good day."

"Thank you for your time." She walks out and closes the door behind her.

I look down at my Maurice Lacroix watch that Cari gave me last Christmas. No one has ever given me a watch as a present. It's the best gift I have ever received, and the most expensive. I know she spent a lot of money on it. Perhaps that's why I wear it often. Who am I kidding? I wear it because it makes me feel close to her even though we're nowhere near each other. There's a beep coming from my laptop to remind me of the next meeting I have in a half hour. I need to let thoughts of Cari go. It's time to prepare for the meeting instead.

~ * ~

THE FOLLOWING DAY

I arrive at the office two hours later than I typically do. I remove my suit jacket and hang it in the closet before heading over to my desk. There's an envelope sitting there with my name typed out. It resembles a resignation letter. I sigh. Who's resigning? I grab the letter opener and open it up. I pull out the piece of paper and my eyes jump to the bottom of the letter first. Shit. It's from Brad. I scan over the letter quickly and throw it down on the desk. Fuck. Despite the fact that I am still somewhat pissed at him, he is excellent at his job and it would be a huge loss for this company if he leaves. My life completely sucks big time.

May has refused to speak to me since the day I found them together. I have done all that I could to avoid Brad over the past couple of weeks, but there's no chance of me avoiding him now. I call Catrina and have her arrange for Brad to come see me. I could have done it myself, but I need a moment to gather my thoughts. The knock on my door takes me away from those thoughts.

"Come in."

"Hey," Brad says.

"Hey," I respond.

He closes my door. He looks unhappy, and I can't imagine it's easy for him to be here right now. Could his unhappiness be because he's not with May? It has been almost a month since he's been with anyone. At least that's what he told me. Has he been with May all this time? He takes a seat in one of the chairs. Before I can even tell him I can't accept his resignation, he speaks first.

"You may not want to hear anything I have to say, but I'm going to say it anyway. I want to apologize and tell you how sorry I am that you had to find out about May and I the way you did. We planned on telling you about us. I want you to know that I am serious about her. I really do care about May. I have no intention of playing with her feelings and treating her like the other girls, but I also value our friendship and don't want to lose it."

Neither do I. Can I trust him not to break my sister's heart? Will he really be good to her? He does seem genuine about his feelings towards her. Perhaps she is what he needs to stop his manwhore ways.

"When did you start developing feelings for her?"

He blows out a puff of air. "Since Christmas."

So it's been a while. Is it right to keep apart two people who want to be together? I know now how difficult it is to be apart from Cari. Perhaps I need to lighten up.

"May is a legal adult, and I really don't have a say in who she can and cannot see."

Brad looks up at me. His eyes are like saucers. Yeah, I'm giving in. It's wrong for me to meddle in their relationship.

"You're fine with me seeing her then?"

I let out a deep breath. "She's heading off to college you know."

"I know. May and I discussed this."

"Are you going to keep seeing her?"

"That's the plan."

"You're not afraid of competition? You are a lot older than some of the guys on campus."

"Love has no age limit."

I narrow my eyes at him. "Do you even know what love is?"

"I'm beginning to get the idea. I understand you're skeptical. I haven't had a steady relationship in a while, but I'm committed to May as long as she wants me." His response surprises me.

"I don't want her heartbroken."

"I have no intentions of breaking her heart."

"I'm going to hold you to it." And I mean it. He really better not hurt her or I will make him pay for it.

"I promise to be good to her."

I reluctantly give him a nod. It will take some getting used to seeing them together, but I do not want to lose either of them. I pick up his resignation letter and wave it in the air.

"Does this have anything to do with May?"

He rubs his cheek. "Yes, it does."

"I see. Do you really want to leave this company?"

"No, I don't."

"Good to know that. I would hate to lose my top guy." I crumple up his letter and toss it in the trash can. "I need you to run this office the next couple of weeks while I am in L.A."

Brad's eyebrow arches. "I'd be glad to, but you're not scheduled to go back next week."

"Something came up and I have to take care of it."

"Got it boss. Is Boston still in the plans for you?"

I am supposed to go with him to Boston in a few weeks to celebrate his grandfather's eightieth birthday. This trip has been planned for months, but there is a part of me that dreads going. How likely will I run into Cari and her new boyfriend? What does he look like? Has she given him her heart? The heart that once belonged to me? Has she given herself to him? *Ugh!* My stomach turns at that thought. I cannot bear to even think about it.

"Yes. That has not changed."

"Great. My family is looking forward to seeing you again." He gets up. "Well, I better get back to work."

"Alright man. I'll catch you later."

"Yeah." He heads towards the door and then turns around. "Want to get a drink after work?"

We haven't gone out for a drink in a while, and I could really use one. "Sure. Why not?"

"Good. I'll stop by at five?"

I give him a nod to confirm. At least things are better with Brad. Now I just have to work on getting May to speak to me.

CHAPTER TEN

DEVEN

I'm at a wedding surrounded by people I do not know. I'm standing in the front waiting for the bride to walk down the aisle. From a distance, I see a vision of white flowing down the aisle. The guests are oohing and aahing over her, and then I catch her hypnotizing eyes. My God, she is absolutely stunning, and takes my breath away. But something does not seem right. Cari walks right past me and stops next to someone I have never seen. He takes her hand and together they walk up to the priest. Who is he and why is this happening? She's not supposed to marry him. I call her name over and over, but she does not turn around. I try to halt things, but no one can hear me. It's as if I'm not there at all.

I awaken startled. My heart is beating unusually fast. I lean back against the headboard and catch my breath. What the fuck was that about? Unable to go back to sleep I put on my gym clothes and begin my workout.

After my morning workout and breakfast, I drove to the cemetery to visit Dad. As I stare down at my father's temporary tombstone, I think of how proud he would be of me now. He would be extremely proud of what I have accomplished. BG finally developed on the other side of the country, and now we are about to make our global mark in Hong Kong. I promised Dad that I will grow the company and so far I am right on track.

Things with May are beginning to get better. She sent me a text last night asking if I would meet her for lunch today. Happy to finally hear from her I agreed to it.

And then there's my pathetic love life. Dad would have called me a fool for letting Cari go. Hell. He doesn't need to call me that. I am a fool for destroying the one good thing I had in my life. I've never been in love before

44

and did not know how strong of an emotion it is. There's no one but her that I want. *No one. She's it for me.* Being apart from her these past few months have been killing me. Dad would have encouraged me to fix things, and make it right. And I think it's about time I do so.

I've been staring at the menu for the past ten minutes as I wait for May at her favorite restaurant in Greenwich.

"Sorry I'm late," May says as she pulls out her chair and sits down.

"It's alright. I'm starving. Know what you want?"

"Yes."

I signal for the server to come over so we can place our orders.

"What's going on May?"

"I asked you out to lunch today so I can thank you for letting Brad and I be together."

I lean back in my chair. "You're eighteen. As much as I'd like to, I can't stop you from seeing who you want."

"No, you can't."

"It's an awkward situation. I don't ever want to have to choose between you and Brad."

"You won't ever have to. We knew what we were getting into, and we both agreed that we would not make you choose if it does not work out between us. We're adults and we'll handle it like adults."

Her words strike me and I realize my baby sister does not need me hovering over her like a protective big brother though I always will. Accepting their relationship is a step in the right direction to fixing things with the both of them.

"So you and Brad, huh?"

"I'm not a baby anymore so start getting used to it."

"I guess I have to. Does he treat you well?"

"Yes, he does. He's so different than the stupid boys in high school."

"High school boys don't mature until later. Sometimes not at all. I want you to be happy."

"Strange you said that because Cari wants me to be happy too."

Hearing May say her name makes my heart clench. "You spoke to Cari?"

"Yes, I did. I called her and told her everything about what happened with Brad, you, and I."

I swallow. "What did she say?" I'm anxious to hear what she told May.

Her eyes narrow. "She told me that by me seeing Brad it would destroy your friendship, and it's not fair to have you choose between us if things don't go well."

Cari and I think so much alike. We are destined to be together. God, how I miss her.

"Did she say anything else?"

May tilts her head. "Like what?" She knows what it is I want to know, but she's going to make me ask it.

"Like how she's doing?"

"No, but I heard some guy call her his baby and she rushed me off the phone."

Jealousy instantly strikes me. She should be with me and not him.

"Are you okay?"

I try to steady my breathing. "Yeah." I need to change the subject. "I'm going back to L.A. for a couple of weeks."

"So soon?"

"There's something I have to take care of."

She eyes me suspiciously. "Such as?"

"It's personal May. I can't get into it."

"You're not going to see that awful bitch Rochelle are you?"

May does not like Rochelle.

"No, I'm not."

"Good. She's not the one for you." I'm well aware of it, but keep that thought to myself. "I don't like her at all Deven."

Just then our lunch is served to us, and we move onto the topic of college as we enjoy our meal. She tells me all that she knows about her roommate. They seem to be a good match for each other, and they both have agreed to meet for dinner next week. It's hard to believe that my baby sister is grown up and will be starting college soon.

CHAPTER ELEVEN

DEVEN

Los Angeles has become my second home. I'm back this time because I must speak to Kaitlin about her current unacceptable relationship, and also about her best friend. She gives me a hug and lets me into her apartment.

"Bourbon?" she asks as I take a seat on her couch.

"Please."

Kait pours some bourbon into a glass, hands it to me, and plops down in the chair across from me.

"So, what is it you want to talk about?"

"You need to put an end to your relationship with Calvin."

"Why? Because you said so?"

"Because it's wrong Kait."

"How is it wrong?"

Kait's been having a relationship with our mother's third husband. I never met him, but I know of him. He is one arrogant son-of-a-bitch. And it is utmostly disgraceful she could engage in such distasteful conduct. For once, I agree with our mother that it's wrong.

"It's incest Kait."

"It is not. We are not blood related."

"He was your stepfather. It's wrong in every way."

"Do you know how many of my friends sleep with their stepfathers?"

What? No, I don't want to know. What kind of friends does she have anyhow?

"TMI. I don't care about what your friends do and don't do. You're *my* sister, and I care about you and your well-being. You're with Rochelle a lot.

What if the paparazzi decide to snoop into your life? Your taboo relationship is going to ruin you and your career. You are too young to let that happen."

She lets out a laugh. I cannot believe she finds this humorous.

"Kait, there is nothing funny about this situation you're in. End the relationship."

"I will not. I love him."

What the fuck does she know about that? "Love? That's not love Kait. It's some sick twisted infatuation."

"It is not. You know not a damn thing about love."

"As a matter of fact, I know a hell of a lot more than you do. I've been in love."

"Yeah. *Been.* And I see how well that worked out for you."

"That's none of your business, okay?"

"Like my relationship with Cal is none of yours either."

This is going to be more difficult than I anticipated. I put down my glass of bourbon, and walk over to the window taking in a few deep breaths.

"If you don't end this relationship with Calvin, I'm going to find him and end it for you."

"You can't do that!"

"I can, and I will. Don't underestimate me Kait."

"You're an asshole."

What is it with my sisters labeling me? "It's not the first time I've been called that. It has to end between the two of you. And you're going to start seeing a shrink."

"*What?!* I don't need to see a shrink."

"Yes, you do."

"You can't tell me what to do."

"You're right. I can't tell you what to do, but I can and will tell you that I do want you to have a happy and normal life. I am concerned about your well-being."

"I am happy and living a normal life."

"Sleeping with your stepfather is in no way normal." I rub my temples. "I don't ask much of anything from you so please just end it with him, and see a shrink. You're going to see how much better your life will be once this is over."

"I'll make a deal with you."

"Let me hear it first."

"I'll end it with Cal if I don't have to go to a shrink."

There's no chance I will agree to that. Each time they argue she goes into a state of deep depression. She would go through days of staying in bed refusing to speak to anyone, starving herself, and not showering. When this has happened in the past, Rochelle and I end up taking turns watching over her. This only continues to bind Rochelle and I together, and I must cut all ties with her.

"Rochelle and I cannot keep coming to your aid. And I also don't want Rochelle to keep thinking she and I are a couple because we're not."

"So this is more about you and not me."

"Wrong. It's about you, but Rochelle ties into my life because of you. I need to tell her once and for all that I am not interested in a relationship with her. So you need to be prepared that she may show her true colors and may no longer want to be your friend."

"You think she will stop being my best friend because you rejected her?"

"Always a possibility."

"Well, if she does then the both of you can go fuck yourselves."

"Then you don't need her as your friend."

"Why Deven?"

"What do you mean why?"

"Why do you hate her? You can't blame her for your break-up."

"Don't start that up again."

"Cari isn't the right girl for you." Who the fuck is she to decide who is and isn't right for me? "She's so insecure that she thought you were cheating on her. I'm so glad Mother said something to her."

I narrow my eyes at her. "When did that happen? I never introduced them to each other."

"At the funeral. Where else?"

I am furious to first learn of this. "Why wasn't I told earlier?"

She shrugs. Fuck. Everything becomes crystal clear now. My mother must have said something to Cari to drive her away before she had a chance to see me. If I had seen her I would have held her in my arms and never let her go. I would have begged her for forgiveness. And now she's in the arms of another man.

"I don't fucking believe this! What did she say to Cari?"

Kait tells all, and I can barely contain my anger. I yell at Kait for taking part in ruining the one thing that truly made me happy. She's never seen me so upset and I can see it frightens her. She looks as if she is about to cry, but I am too angry to care about her emotional state. I turn my back to her and storm out of her apartment.

CHAPTER TWELVE

DEVEN

Leaning over the railing on the pier, I look out towards the golden horizon. People are enjoying their lives like they should be while my personal life is nothing but a disaster. I pull out my phone and send an email to my mother letting her know that I am officially cutting all ties with her. What she did to Cari is unforgivable. It's over. Dad's gone, and I'm done with her. She no longer has a place in my life.

I scroll through the photos on my phone which are mostly of Cari. I never could bring myself to delete these pictures I have of her. She's my anchor. My soul mate. She's perfect for me. Letting her go was my mistake. I reacted out of pure jealousy and let it cloud my rational thoughts. If only I had given her a chance to explain then we could have talked it over and worked on the trust issues. I blamed her for destroying our euphoric world when all along it was I who destroyed it. I should have come forward and told her about Kait's taboo relationship, and explained how it tied me to Rochelle.

"Excuse me."

I turn around to see a pretty girl who is probably not older than twenty ogling me. Ugh!

"My friends and I think you're so cute." I look over to her friends who are also ogling me. "Would you mind taking a group picture of us?"

I shrug. "Sure."

She hands me her phone and I focus in on the picture. I take the snapshot and hand the phone back to the girl. She takes the phone and lingers. Here it comes.

"We're going to get some drinks. Would you like to join us?"

So damn predictable. "Not interested."

The girl's jaw dropped open and I hear one of them mumble that if I change my mind I can still join them. I don't catch the name of where they are heading off to, but it doesn't matter. I'm not joining them.

I look back down at my phone and scroll through my contact list and see Cari's information. My finger hovers over her number as I debate whether or not to call her. No, a phone call won't do. I need to see her in person. I scroll down a little further and call the one person who is able to help me, but may be reluctant to do so.

"What do you want?" the hostile voice asks on the other line. I deserve that after hurting Cari.

"How are you Rodrigo?"

"I'm fine and dandy. I would ask how you are doing, but I know you are doing good."

"I'm not sure where you got that information from, but I'm not doing good."

"Oh? What happened? Your movie star actress dumped your sorry ass?"

Damn. I am really on his shit list. How in the world does Cari get along with him? They are complete opposites. "No. If you are implying that I was seeing her you're mistaken. I have been with no one since Cari."

"That's not what I have seen and heard."

"Whatever it is you have seen and heard is incorrect. I want Cari back and I need your assistance."

Rodrigo laughs and I hear Hunter's voice in the background, but I can't make out what he is saying.

"You're a douchebag, and you want my help? You broke her heart. She had a hard time trusting men after what the other douchebag did to her, and then she met you. You were the first guy she actually wanted to be with in years and yet you come from the same class of douches as the other one did. She is not a malicious person. She is the most kind-hearted person I know, and for you to go and accuse her -"

That's enough. I cut him off. "I was wr-"

He cuts me off in return. "You don't get to speak until I am done. You accused her of cheating without even giving her a chance to explain. Are you that stupid and insecure to think she would cheat on you? Cari is faithful. She's nothing like the cheap sluts you have been with. She fell in love with you and what do you do? You chose to dump her like she was a piece of trash. She fell apart because of you. Thank God Hunter, Zach, Alana, and I helped her to pick up the pieces.

"She's had a lot of loss in her life. I was by her side when she lost her grandparents. She was heartbroken then, but nothing...nothing was worse than watching her cry over you and losing the baby..." His voice breaks. Baby? Did he just say baby?

"What baby? What the fuck are you talking about?"

"Oh shit."

"What baby Rodrigo?"

"Damn my big mouth. I hope Cari forgives me for telling you. She found out she was pregnant after your father's funeral."

My mind is reeling from this information. It had to be my baby. "Was it mine?"

"You *are* a douche. Of course it was yours! Do you think Cari is the type of lady that sleeps around?"

Of course not! "Why didn't she tell me?"

"Because you're a piece of sh-"

I don't let him say the word. I know what I am, but she should have told me she was pregnant.

"I had the right to know."

"Well, I can't disagree with you on that. You were her first love, and *you* left her heartbroken. You don't deserve her. I'm so glad she's moved on and seeing someone new."

The reminder that she is with someone else continues to pierce my heart. He's right. I don't deserve her after how I treated her, but I'm selfish and refuse to give up on her. "I was wrong to have let her go, but I care about Cari more than anyone else."

"Did you not listen when I said she's seeing someone?"

"I listened, but she was mine first."

"Well, you royally screwed that up."

"I know, and I regret it. I was going to ask her to marry me."

"Excuse me?"

I let out a huff of breath. "When I was in L.A. right before Christmas, I had a custom-designed ring made just for her."

"What a shame that it's too late. She's better off now anyway without you."

Damn him. He is not making this easy. "Please Rodrigo. I need you to help me."

"I have to do no such thing. You were supposed to be her happy ever after."

"I still want to be her happy ever after."

"Too late. She's moved on. Don't go messing up her new life." He's being quite impossible, but I understand why so I allow him to say what he has to say. Best to let him get it off his chest. I hear Hunter again in the background, and this time around I can make out what he is saying. He's telling Rodrigo to hear me out. I owe Hunter one. Rodrigo lets out a loud sigh. "Fine. I can't promise that she will give you the time of day."

I promise him I will never hurt her again. And I mean it. Rodrigo only gives me her work information. He refuses to give me her home address claiming it is for her protection. I cannot get mad at him for that because he is watching out for her and I appreciate how he always looks out for her even though my intentions are far from hurting her.

"If you ever hurt her again, you will answer to me."

If I hurt her again, I don't deserve to be happy ever. And then there is the baby she lost. *Our baby.* I close my eyes briefly thinking about how alone she must have felt. I should have been there with her when it happened. This is all my doing and a lifetime of making it up to her will never compensate for everything I put her through.

CHAPTER THIRTEEN

DEVEN

Kait has been trying to reach me the past week, but I ignore every single one of her calls. There is nothing left that I have to say to her. My phone beeps again and I see Ken's number on the screen.

"Ken."

"Hey Deven."

"If you're going to tell me again how sorry Kait is I will end this call now."

"No, I'm not. She deserves to feel like shit after what she pulled." Ken has sided with me after I told him what I learned. He was fond of Cari and when I gave him the news it was over he called me a dumbass for letting her go.

"What's up?"

"I got some news for you."

"What is it?"

"You're an uncle."

I'm an uncle? What is he talking about?

"Deven?"

"I'm still here. What do you mean by I am an uncle? Please tell me you got a dog."

He laughs. "No, it's better. I have a daughter."

WTF?

"You have a daughter?"

"Yeah, I do. Got the DNA results and it proves that I am her daddy."

"That's huge news."

"It is."

"Who else knows?"

"Just you and Kait. Dev, she's beautiful just like her mother."

Ken launches into the story of how he and the mother of his child met. He tells me all about his daughter, Mandy. She's four years old and loves animals. Ken wants to make the guest room into her room. I listen to him talk about what he wants to do, but I know he does not have the money to decorate and furnish it. As my gift to my niece, I offer to take care of decorating and furnishing her room.

A few days later, I am back at their apartment to meet my niece. Ken hasn't returned yet with Mandy so I'm left alone with Kait.

"I'm sorry Deven for everything," Kait says first. She should be sorry. Her meddling in my personal relationship was uncalled for. I never wanted my past with Rochelle to affect what I had with Cari. "I didn't know how much Cari meant to you and how much you loved her."

Love her. I still love her. I don't know what she expects me to say.

"I did a lot of thinking about what you said, and I ended things with Cal." Well, thank God for that. "And I'll go see a shrink. I made an appointment for next Wednesday."

"Very well."

"I also spoke to Rochelle. I explained that you're not interested in her other than being a friend." *No. I wanted to cut all ties.* "She admitted to me she is jealous of Cari. She feels that Cari stole you from her." These girls do not get it. "But she didn't say she wanted to stop being friends with me, so that's a positive thing, right?"

"Whatever suits the both of you."

"I'm really sorry Deven. What can I do to make you no longer mad at me?"

I close my eyes and draw in a deep breath. When I open my eyes, I stare right at her.

"There's nothing more you can do. You will move on with your life and hopefully you will see that I have been right all along about everything I have said to you. Don't ever get involved in my personal life again. Do you understand?"

She nods. "Can I ask you something?"

"Depends on the question."

"Have you tried to talk to Cari?"

"How can I? Your mother pushed Cari right out of my arms and into the arms of another man."

"She's your mother too."

"No. She no longer is my mother. I have severed my relationship with her. What she did was completely unforgivable."

Her mouth opens wide from shock, but nothing comes out. Just then Ken returns with Mandy. Wow! She is cute with blonde curls, large hazel eyes, and a little turned up nose. She seems terrified and clings tightly to Ken. Kait approaches her first.

"Hi Mandy. I'm your Aunt Kaitlin. Welcome to your new home." The little girl does not respond to Kait. "We're going to have lots and lots of fun. Look at what I have for you." Kait pulls out a lollipop from her pocket. Oh that's just great. Bribe her with candy. Way to win her over.

Mandy looks at Kait and slowly reaches out for the lollipop. She whispers something to Kait.

"This is Uncle Deven."

I kneel down so I am eye-to-eye with her. "Hi Mandy. It's nice to meet you. We have a surprise for you. Would you like to see it?" She does not respond to my question and still seems scared and shy. I lead the way to her new bedroom. The interior designer I hired to decorate the room did a fantastic job and quickly too. I love when money talks.

"Do you like Dora?" She nods her head. "Good. Your room is full of Dora." She doesn't budge. I look up at Ken and he pulls her with him to her new room.

I thought she would have been jumping up and down as soon as she saw her room, but she just stands there and looks around. There is no smile on her face. Christ, she's one tough kid to charm.

Ken bends down and says something to her. He lets go of her hand and she takes small steps towards me. I ask her if she would like to meet Dora, and she nods her head. I suggest a trip to Universal Studios and her cute face lights up with a smile. I open my arms and she comes into them wrapping her little arms around me. Hugging her makes me long to have a kid of my own. And I think of the baby I didn't even know about and hug my niece tightly. Life really is so precious.

CHAPTER FOURTEEN

Early September

DEVEN

After leaving California, I spent a couple of days in the Caribbean on a private island to gather my thoughts and set forth my plan. Before returning to New York a few nights ago, Mom asked if I could stay over at the house before May leaves for college. Knowing it would mean everything to her to have her children under the same roof, I agree to it. She'll soon have an empty house.

Finding it impossible to fall asleep, I get out of bed and head down to the kitchen. I am startled to see Mayleen sitting at the kitchen table when I turn the lights on.

"Hey. What are you doing up?" I ask scratching the back of my head.

"I couldn't sleep. You neither?"

"Yeah." I sit down across from her. "What's keeping you up?"

"I miss Dad. I wish he was seeing me off tomorrow." She sighs and her shoulders slump.

"So do I."

"I want to ask you a question."

"Yeah, of course."

"Do you miss Cari?"

I look out the window and stare into the darkness outside.

"I do."

"Do you still love her?"

I do. I have been denying my feelings all these months when I should have chased after her and not let so much time pass by. "Yes, very much. Why the question May? Did you speak to her again?"

She shakes her head. "Not since I last told you, but there was something in her voice the last time I spoke to her."

"What do you mean by that?"

"I think she still cares about you."

I hope so. "Did she tell you that?"

"Sort of."

I am anxious to know what Cari told her. "What did she say?"

"She said she will always care about you."

The fact that she will always care about me speaks volumes. "She did?"

"Yeah. Ever since you two split up you have been working like crazy as if it's the only thing you have." May has a bad habit of reminding me of this. "When you were with Cari, you were happier and just…" She shrugs. "Nicer."

Nicer? Huh, I have never been told that. However, Cari did make me happy.

"When you were with her, you were the happiest I had ever seen you." She gets up from her seat and gives me a hug. "We don't always get second chances. I love you, and I hope you take a chance and try to make things right again between the two of you. Don't wait too long otherwise you will lose her for good." She releases me and starts to walk away.

"How did my baby sister get to be so smart about relationships?"

"I'm not. I had hoped someday you and Cari would end up getting married. I would have loved to have her as my sister-in-law. Well, off to bed I go. I have a big day tomorrow. Good night."

"Good night."

I stay in the kitchen reflecting back on the memories I had with Cari. I think about how she was the one for me, and how she still is the one for me.

~ * ~

The next morning we leave early for Princeton and I manage to get an hour's rest on the drive down since Brad was doing the driving. Cars park where they can to unload, and I have Mauricio do the same.

"What do you have in here?" Brad asks May as he and Mauricio carry her Louis Vuitton trunk case towards her dorm.

"My shoes of course."

My eyes widen in shock. *"What?!"*

"I couldn't decide which pairs I would need so I packed most of them." Without exaggeration, my baby sister has at least a hundred pairs of shoes. I shake my head at her shoe infatuation.

We had already packed Leigh's Land Rover with two large suitcases and the trunk case. I had another two suitcases in my Porsche, and Mauricio had three more suitcases in the new Mercedes S600.

I grab a suitcase and so does May. She leads the way to her room. The halls are crowded and we all do our best to maneuver through the chaos to get to her room. Her roommate is unpacking when we arrive. May introduces us. She's from Nashville, and another one who can't seem to take her eyes off of Brad and I. She stutters as she tries to speak. May will need to break the news to her roomie that I am not interested in her.

Once May seems to be somewhat settled in, it's time for us to go. Mom is crying and May immediately gives her a hug as she cries along with her. When they finally let go of each other May looks at me with wet eyes.

"Come here," I say as I open my arms. I hug her. "Be safe. Be good."

"I will."

"Don't party too much."

She laughs. "Promise."

"I'm always a phone or text away."

"I know. Don't give up hope, and take a chance." She's referencing to Cari.

"I'm going to give it a shot."

"Good. I'll miss you."

I kiss the top of her head and release her. She walks away from Mom and I, and goes to Brad. I watch the two of them. I envy what they have because it's something I once had with Cari. May turns back to me and I know that's my cue to exit with Mom.

"We'll leave you both alone. Brad, I'll wait for you outside," I say grabbing the empty suitcases so I can take them back to the car.

"Be there in a bit."

I sent Mom home first with Mauricio following behind. I sit down on a bench and read my emails while I wait for Brad. Done with the emails, I look at the photos I have of Cari. I miss her beautiful smile, her soft laughter, her warm body pressed to mine. I fucking miss her. I need her back in my life.

"Ready?"

I look up. It's Brad. Huh. He actually looks sad.

"Are you going to be okay?"

He shrugs. "I hope so. There are a lot of guys her age on campus."

Confident ex-manwhore Brad is feeling insecure? Now that's a first. I have never known him to feel insecure.

"Afraid she's going to be whisked away by some college guy?"

"Yeah, I am."

Whoa. Maybe he's more into May than I thought.

"May likes you a lot."

"But she's still young."

Yes, she is. And I had pointed out the age difference to him. As much as I would love to rub it in his face that I told him so, I can't bring myself to do so. I, of all people, know the feeling of what it's like to not be with the girl of your dreams. But I also know my sister. She's had a thing for him for quite some time so she will remain loyal to him. I stand up and we start to walk to my car.

"Take it one day at a time Brad. It's taken so long for you and her to get to this point."

"Expert advice?"

"On the contrary. You and May have known each other for years."

"I wish we had more time together before she started school."

"You can make up for the lost time. She's close enough that you two can spend the weekends together."

"Yeah. I was thinking of asking her to come to Boston for my grandfather's birthday so I can officially introduce her to the rest of my family."

He's definitely serious about her. It's a good plan, and will give me a chance to seek Cari out on my own. I haven't mentioned my plan to Brad. Perhaps I should do so now.

"Speaking of Boston, I am going to try to find Cari."

Brad stops a few feet from my car.

"Really?"

"Yep."

"Finally listening to your heart?"

I nod. "I made a massive mistake and I need her to see that."

"It's about time. You two are meant for each other."

"I couldn't agree with you more. And I need your help so I can make it right."

"You got it. Whatever you need man."

I tell him my plan and he agrees to help me. Now all I have to do is get to Boston and find Cari.

CHAPTER FIFTEEN

DEVEN

I have been counting down the days until our trip to Boston, and the day has finally come. Brad and I leave work early to start on our road trip. May will take a flight to Boston tomorrow afternoon after she is done with her last class of the day. Driving together to Boston reminds me of our college days when we used to take weekend road trips. I arranged for us to meet up with some friends from college at the POSH tonight. We haven't seen them since we all graduated.

We get to Boston by three, and check into the hotel where we will be staying. Even though we traveled together in the same car, we booked separate rooms. I am on my laptop and work until sometime into the early morning hours, and I certainly do not want to have to listen to Brad and May. Brad could have stayed at his parents' house, but with May coming he wanted her to stay with him. The only way they can be together is in a hotel room. His parents are old school and having her stay in their home is not permitted. I didn't think Brad would ever settle with one girl, but he has. I will never admit it to him, but I guess I have been proven wrong. He treats my sister like a princess and he really adores her. And she's over the moon for him.

I meet Brad back in the lobby and we walk over to the POSH hotel which is only a few blocks away. I intentionally selected the POSH as our meeting place after learning from Rodrigo that Cari works there. I hope my plan to see her again goes accordingly.

Brad and I are the first to arrive. One by one, our friends trickle in and join us. It's great to see them. The five of us order drinks and catch up. Each of them is seeing someone except for me. Yeah, I'm the big loser, but hopefully not for long. As we continue to drink and chat, I receive a call from Catrina. I step into the lobby to take the call.

"Yes, Catrina?"

She asks me for my approval on an advance for the renovations to the abandoned Tribeca building I purchased and plan to transform into loft apartments. I lean against the wall listening to her as she updates me on what has happened since I left.

"I'll approve two and a half million, but you tell Larry that if he can't agree to that then everything will be negated. This has -"

I lose my train of thought when I see from a distance the back of someone wearing a familiar blue dress. She turns, and my heart skips a few beats. *Fuck me.*

"I'll have to call you back Catrina." I end the call and follow the lady in blue.

~ * ~

CARI

I clear off my desk and grab my bag to leave. Grady is away at a conference in San Diego so Faith and I made plans to have dinner tonight. I meet Faith in her office and we walk through the lobby towards the main entrance passing by the bar which is busy as usual. POSH has one of the trendiest bars in Boston.

"Cari?"

I hear my name and spin around. I see a stunning man coming towards me. Who is *he*? And how does he know my name? As he comes closer to me, my mouth drops open. I can never forget those piercing cerulean eyes. *Oh. My. God.* I struggle to catch my breath. Gone is the long hair that I loved so much. He's now sporting a shorter layered tousled hairstyle. His face is scruffy and he looks like he hasn't slept in days yet he still manages to look gorgeous. How is it legal for a man to look so hot?

"Holy hotness! Who's hunkalicious?" Faith whispers not taking her eyes off of Deven.

"Um, that's Deven. My ex."

"He's delicious."

Deven seems to have put back the weight he lost several months ago when I last saw him at his father's funeral making him look much healthier.

"I think he wants to speak to you. Do you want me to stay with you?"

I don't want her to leave me, but I don't want her to stand there and gawk at my ex-boyfriend either. "Thanks, but I think it's better if I speak to him alone."

"Got it. He's a dish. You two make a gorgeous couple. I don't know how you could let him go."

It was him who let me go, but she doesn't know that. She has been under the assumption that we broke up because I took this job. "Call me if you need me to come back and rescue you. We'll have dinner another night."

"Thanks."

"See you tomorrow then."

"I'll see you tomorrow."

As she walks away, Deven stops in front of me. The electricity between us is still there and undeniable.

"I thought it was you."

My eyes take him in, but my voice fails me.

He gives me a half smile. "How have you been?"

I swallow. "I've been good. And you?"

He shrugs. "As well as can be." His tone suggests anything but.

I avert my gaze to my shoes. "What are you doing in Boston?"

"Look at me Cari." Just like old times, I do as he requests. I lift my head to see his piercing blue eyes burn through me. "I can ask you the same, but I have a feeling I know the answer."

Of course he does. *He knows everything.* "I work here."

He crosses his arms. "And I'm here with Brad. He invited me to come to Boston to celebrate his grandfather's birthday on Saturday. I suggested we make a long weekend out of it so we drove up today. We're meeting some old college buddies at the bar."

"Oh." Being so close to him is making the feelings I had suppressed for him resurface. I must not let it happen. It's not fair to Grady.

Neither of us says another word. The silence between us is awkward.

"I was wondering if you're not doing anything tomorrow night after work maybe we could have dinner and catch up?"

"Um…" I'm torn by his offer. No. I can't. I should not consider his offer at all. "I had plans to go out for drinks with some of my co-workers."

"Oh. I see. I mean I understand. It's Friday after all. Why wouldn't you have plans? Maybe another time then." My heart sinks when I notice the disappointment on his face and in his voice. Will there be another time? "I better get back. It was good to see you again."

We remain standing there staring at each other. His eyes look sad. I want nothing more than to hold him. I don't want him to go. If I let him walk away I may never see him again. I need to say something.

"I'll change my plans for tomorrow." Did I just really say that?

His lips curl into a smile. "Yeah?"

"Yes. There will be other Fridays I can go out with them."

He's about to reach for my hand, but retracts.

"Thank you Cari. Why don't I meet you outside the entrance after work?"

"That will be great. I get out at five tomorrow."

"I'll be waiting."

"Okay. I, um, should go now."

"Right. Me too. See you tomorrow then."

I give him a nod and leave. Tomorrow cannot come soon enough.

CHAPTER SIXTEEN

CARI

The anticipation of having dinner with Deven kept me up all night, and butterflies have been fluttering around in my stomach throughout the day. I spent an hour this morning picking out an outfit, and then another half hour fixing my hair and putting on my make-up. I feel silly for getting all dolled up. It's not as if we are going out on a date. I thought I had gotten over my feelings for him, but seeing him again reconfirms that I'm not over him yet. Will I ever be?

Deven is waiting for me outside of the hotel like he said he would. He gives me his swoon worthy dimpled smile, and my heart stops beating for a moment.

"Hi." He steps next to me and leans in like he's going to kiss me on the cheek, but pulls back instead leaving me disappointed.

"Hi."

"Do you have a preference for dinner?"

"Oh, not at all."

We decide on a restaurant on Newbury Street, and start walking in that direction.

"How do you like working at the hotel?"

"I like it a lot."

"Better than BG?"

How do I answer that question? I just need to be fair and honest. I look at him. "I liked working at BG."

He looks back at me and there's a twinkle in those beautiful blue eyes of his. "Do you miss New York?"

I miss the people in New York. A city is a city. It's the people I am surrounded by that makes living in the city enjoyable.

"I do."

"Do you ever think about going back?"

"There's no reason for me to go back. Rodrigo and Hunter are living together, and it's more expensive to live there than here."

He doesn't reply and we continue our walk in silence through the Boston Public Garden. I don't want him to ask any more questions that will make me feel uneasy.

"How is everything going in L.A., and Seattle?"

"It's going well. We're making a lot of progress. I also have a team heading over to Hong Kong to begin work there."

He acquired property in Hong Kong? "Hong Kong is a done deal?"

"Yeah. It finally is."

I am so very happy for him. Instinctively I hug him, but quickly pull away. Oh my God. I should not have done that.

"That's really wonderful Deven. You're making your global mark like you wanted to."

"Well, it's part of my global expansion plan." He smiles and I cannot help myself from smiling either as I remember my question to him on our first date.

"Your father would have been so proud of you."

"Yeah, I believe so."

"I'm sorry about your father. I know how much he meant to you."

"Thank you Cari." We stop at the bridge and watch as people get onto the swan boats. "I miss him very much." He rakes his fingers through his hair messing it up and making him look even sexier. I must stop staring at him.

"I was in L.A. when I got the call. It finally hit me that I was losing him. I suddenly became scared. I wasn't ready for him to go no matter how much I prepared myself mentally for it. I wanted to speak to you. You were the first person I wanted to call because I knew you would understand what I was going through."

"You should have called me."

"I should have."

He should have, but he didn't and we both know why. My eyes fall to his wrist and to the watch he has on. It's the watch I gave him for Christmas.

"It's my favorite watch. I wear it often," he says when he catches me staring at it.

His admission pleases me, but I won't let him know that. Does he think of me each time he wears it?

I turn my attention back to the boat. "How are Leigh, and Mayleen?"

"Leigh is good. She finally took some time for herself and went to Europe. May is at Princeton, and she's dating Brad."

"She called me and told me about their relationship. How do you feel about them together?"

"At first, I was angry. My sister and my best friend shacking up? I felt betrayed, but as time passed, I came to realize they both like each other a lot. And they're both adults. Who am I to get in the way of their blossoming relationship?"

"You gave them your blessing?"

"Reluctantly I did. Who could have known that my baby sister would be the one to bring Brad to his knees?" We both chuckle simultaneously because we know how much of a womanizer Brad was.

We continue to catch up over dinner talking as if time never passed. After dinner he walks me back home. As we near my apartment, I dread having to say good-bye to him. I don't want him to leave yet. Being with him tonight has evoked happiness…the same happiness I once had with him. But it can't be. That happiness no longer exists. He made his choice and he chose Rochelle.

"It's a nice neighborhood you chose to live in."

"I think so. Would you like to come inside?"

Without hesitation he responds to my offer with a nod and a smile, and follows me in.

"I like your place."

"Thanks. Rodrigo and Hunter helped."

"Of course. They're great friends."

"Yes, they are."

"What are your neighbors like?"

"There is a family that lives on the first floor and they seem to be nice. I hardly see the guy that lives above me." I step into the kitchen. "Coffee?"

"Yes. I'd love a cup."

I place the coffee grinds into the coffee machine and press the start button. When I turn around to reach for two cups from the cabinet I see he is no longer in the kitchen and has wandered off into the living room.

˜ * ˜

DEVEN

Her apartment is much smaller than the one she had in New York City, but it's clean and comfortable. I step into her living room and look at the various picture frames she has on her shelves. There's a picture of her standing in a front of a guy whose arms are wrapped around her. I pick up the picture frame and stare at it. He must be the guy she is seeing. They appear quite happy, and it makes me want to rip him apart.

"Deven?"

I turn around and she notices the heart shaped frame in my hands. I point to the picture. She looks just as beautiful in the picture as she does in person.

"Where was this taken?"

"At a friend's engagement party."

"And who's the lucky guy?"

"Someone I am seeing." She purses her lips. I knew that was coming, but it does not hurt any less to hear her say it.

"What's his name?"

"Grady," she responds quickly and bites down on her bottom lip.

What kind of name is that? "I hope he's treating you well."

"He is."

"Good. You deserve to be treated well."

I place the picture back on the shelf, but something else catches my eye. It's a frame with the inscription "Love at First Sight." In it is a sonogram picture. My eyes shift to the tiered wooden block beside it.

Baby Snow Blake
Our angel
Forever missed
Forever in our hearts

My eyes dart back to the sonogram picture. I hold the frame and look at the picture of our baby. I look back at her. Her eyes are filled with pain, and tears flow down her anguished face.

She wipes them away with the back of her hand. "Our baby."

Our baby. Little does she know that I have been made aware she was pregnant.

"Why didn't you tell me?"

She shakes her head. "I wanted to."

"So why didn't you?"

"You were with Rochelle, and I didn't want you to think I was using the baby as an excuse to get you back."

Hearing her say that is like taking a punch in the gut. *Deep breath Blake.*

"I never would have thought that."

"How could I have known?"

"I had every right to know."

She nods. "You did, and I'm sorry. I should have told you."

"Did you know you were pregnant when we broke up?"

She shakes her head. "No. I found out sometime after your father's funeral."

"Cari, there's something I have to clear up. I was never with Rochelle or anyone else after we broke up."

She looks at me in disbelief. *Yeah, angel. It's true. My heart has been yours from the moment we met.*

"I thought…"

"Did you think I could really move on after you?" My voice is an octave higher.

She seems taken aback. "I saw how cozy the two of you were at the restaurant after the funeral."

My mind travels back to that day, but I can't seem to remember ever being cozy with Rochelle. "I don't recall being 'cozy' with her."

"It doesn't matter anymore, does it?"

She's wrong. "It will always matter with you."

She looks down at the hardwood floor while crossing her arms. "I saw your arm around her."

Do we really have to discuss this? "That day was a rough one for me, but I can assure you that it meant nothing. I told you before there has been nothing going on between her and I for a long time." She gives me a nod as if finally accepting that I'm telling her the truth. "How far along where you when you lost the baby?"

"Thirteen weeks."

My knees feel like they're going to buckle. I struggle to catch my breath. Why has God been so cruel to me? I lost my father, and our baby within a matter of months. Anger and hurt run through me, but I fight hard to contain my emotions.

"What caused the miscarriage?"

"I wanted our baby more than anything, but my body wasn't ready for a baby. When I lost our baby, I felt quite alone. Even though Rodrigo was there to comfort me it just wasn't the same. I wanted you there with me." She covers her face and weeps into her hands. I take a step closer and pull her into my arms. Her hands fall from her face. She buries her face in my chest, and her arms immediately wrap around me. We stand there holding each other tightly. I close my eyes wishing things had been different. She should have told me about the pregnancy. I would have been there for her. My heart aches as much as hers does for our lost child. I kiss the top of her head.

When her crying slows, she pulls back and stares at my shirt. "I'm sorry I got your shirt all wet."

"It'll dry." I tip her face up so I can look into her eyes. The sadness in her eyes mirrors the sadness in mine. I move my hands and frame her face. Alarms and bells are sounding off in my head warning me not to go through with this, but I ignore all of it. I gently kiss the corners of her semi-wet eyes and then move my lips down her cheek until our lips meet. Her lips move with mine. God, how I've missed her. She pulls back from the kiss first. Our foreheads touch and she puts her palms on my chest. I close my hand around one of hers.

"I missed you so much. I never ever stopped loving you. You're all I ever think about. I tried hard to forget you, but I just couldn't," I admit.

"I missed you too, but you, me…we can't do this." She shakes her head. "It's not fair to Grady."

My happy heart nosedives to the floor. Fucking Grady. No. Fuck Grady. I felt how she responded to me in that kiss. She still feels something for me, and I'll be damned if she denies it and I don't do something about it. It's not the end for us. Fate is playing with us again.

"If I never let you go in the first place we wouldn't be here now would we?"

"We can't go backwards." She nibbles on her lower lip.

"No, we can't. But I do owe you an explanation."

"An explanation?"

I run my fingers through my hair and then slide my hands into the pockets of my pants.

"I made a mistake the day I let you go. I should have been forthcoming and told you what was going on."

She shakes her head. "You lost me Deven."

"Do you remember when I told you that Kait was dealing with some issues?"

"Yes, I remember."

"She was having a relationship with her stepfather." Her eyes widen and her mouth opens wide. I expected her reaction to be as such.

"Her stepfather?"

"Yes. He married *her* mother after the divorce." I know it didn't pass her by when I don't acknowledge *her* as my mother. Cari is bright and she'll be able to pick up on my connotation. "They had been together a year before they were caught. You can imagine the shock when we found out. The family tried to break up their relationship, but it only made things worse and became more complicated. Kait became very depressed." I shudder at those memories, but press on. "After that we sought help for her, and slowly she started to get herself together. That's when she decided she wanted to go into acting and it's through acting school that she met her best friend, Rochelle. Rochelle has been the one who has helped to watch over her especially when she got back together with that asshole stepfather of hers."

She doesn't say anything for a while. She's probably disgusted to learn the ugly truth. "Why didn't you tell me about this earlier?"

I am not holding anything back this time. "I wanted to. Believe me I did, but I just couldn't do it. I can't tell you how much I wish could turn back the hands of time, but it's all over now. I gave Kait an ultimatum, and she has finally ended the relationship. And she also made it clear to Rochelle that I am not interested in her."

"Why are you telling me all of this now?"

"Because you deserve nothing but the truth, and I'm begging for your forgiveness."

She purses her lips, and I hate that I don't know what she is thinking. "The day you ended things you said there was no trust."

"I was wrong."

"But you weren't. You didn't trust me enough to tell me about Rochelle, and you didn't trust me when I told you that Zach is only a friend. You didn't give me a chance to explain. He was only comforting me when you came back. It was nothing more. You crushed me and tossed away our relationship like it was trash."

"I can't express how truly sorry I am. I was overcome with jealousy and overreacted."

She draws in a long breath and lets it out. "It's all water under the bridge. I've moved on."

Nuh-uh. She *thinks* she's moved on, but that kiss told me something entirely different.

"No." I shake my head. She looks at me with disbelief. "You still have feelings for me. I felt it when you kissed me."

She opens her mouth to say something, but closes it instead. I lay my hands gently on her shoulders and look into her somber eyes. "You are a kind person and it's not in you to hurt people. I am not over you and I never will

be. I'm going to fight for you, and win you back because we belong together."
She shakes her head. I'm not giving up on us. "I never cheated on you nor
would I ever. My heart belongs to you. It has from the first moment we were
together at the club."

Her eyes are glassy. "I can't do this. It's too late."

I drop my hands from her shoulder and take in a deep breath. Oh fuck
no. "It's never too late. I love you Cari. I've never stopped loving you. Do you
know what I see in my future?" She shakes her head. "I see you. I see us.
You're it for me. Always have been, and always will be."

She places her hand over her mouth and shakes her head. "No. Please
don't say that." A tear rolls down her cheek.

"How can I not?"

"It's impossible."

"No, Cari. I don't believe that at all. *It is possible.*" I reach for her hand,
but she moves it behind her back.

"I'm sorry Deven."

Nothing is going to stop me from trying to win her back. I will do
whatever I have to in order to prove my love for her. If she asks me to run
around the block in my underwear, I will. If she asks me to declare to the
world that I was an asshole to her from the top of the Empire State Building,
I will do that too. I will do *anything* to win her back. I need to find a way to
make it right between us again no matter what it takes.

"Fine Cari. I'll let it be for now, but this is not the end for us," I tell her
as I walk out the door.

CHAPTER SEVENTEEN

CARI

I lean against the door and close my eyes. I should not have kept the news about the baby from him. He did have a right to know. My mind goes back to the kiss. The moment our lips touched my feelings for him resurrected. I finally started to make progress with moving on and his admission of his unrequited love leaves me disconcerted. Why did he have to come back now and complicate my life?

The ringtone coming from my phone distracts me from my thoughts and I go over to answer the call. I look down at the screen and see Grady's number. I can't possibly speak to him now. Not when my feelings for Deven have reemerged. It's not fair to him. But I can't even think about Grady right now as my thoughts are all of Deven. After all these months, he finally told me the truth. The truth that should have been told to me the day things fell apart. It's scandalous what Kait has been doing, but now I get it. I get all of it now. My phone rings again. This time I don't bother to see who's calling before answering it.

"Hi sweetie."

"Hi Rodrigo. I was planning to call you later."

"Well, I beat you to it. What's wrong sweetie? You don't sound too happy. Did something happen with Grady?"

He would be a lot easier to deal with. "No. It's Deven."

"Deven?"

"He's here in Boston."

"He really did go."

Rodrigo knew? "Did you know he was coming to Boston?"

Rodrigo confesses he is the one who told Deven where I could be found, and explains to me why he felt he had to help Deven. After listening to his confession, I am uncertain whether I should thank him or not.

"Now it's your turn to tell me what happened." And I do tell him. "Oh my God. You are still in love him aren't you?"

"Yes. And I wish I could stop the feeling."

"Why do you wish that?"

"It's not fair to Grady." Hurting Grady is the last thing I want to do.

"Let me give you some advice. You cannot worry about how Grady or Deven will feel. One of them will end up getting hurt when you choose who you want to be with. You deserve a happy ever after so pick the person who you know will make you happy."

How can there be a happy ever after if someone is going to end up getting hurt?

~ * ~

DEVEN

I give the bartender my order for another whiskey. Tonight did not end the way I had wanted it to, but I'm not giving up on us. I meant what I said. I will fight for her and make her see that we belong together.

A lifetime of making it up to her will not compensate for everything I put her through. I should have been honest with her from the very beginning about Kait, and Rochelle. I cannot undo what's already been done, but I can show her what a good future we can still have together. She's my once in a lifetime. And without her, my life is empty and means nothing.

"Everything all right man?" Brad eyes my drink. I texted him earlier to meet me here after he took May up to his room. I didn't want May to know yet that I had been with Cari tonight.

"I saw Cari tonight."

"How did it go?" Brad takes the seat beside me and orders himself a drink.

"Not the way I had hoped."

"What happened?"

"It didn't go the way I thought it would, but when I kissed her and she kissed me back, I knew for sure she still has feelings for me."

He looks at me like I am donning the scarlet letter. "You kissed her knowing she's with someone else?"

"Yeah, I did." Brad has no idea what lead to the kiss so I tell him. "There's something else. She was pregnant."

Brad gives me an incredulous look. "What?"

"You heard me. And before you ask the next question, the baby was mine."

"Was?"

"She miscarried."

"Oh man. I'm really sorry."

"So am I." I would have loved having a baby with her.

"It must suck to find out now."

"You have no idea," I say and take a big swallow of my whiskey.

"Why didn't she tell you?"

I let out a deep sigh. "She thought I had moved on with Rochelle."

"No way."

"Yeah."

"I don't know how she came to that conclusion. Cari is a hundred times hotter than Rochelle, and she is the sweetest thing in the world. You and Cari should be together."

"I can't agree with you more. I'm not giving up on her, or us. I'm going to get her back."

He slaps my back. "I know you will."

I have to. She's my world.

CHAPTER EIGHTEEN

DEVEN

I take Mom out for brunch at her favorite restaurant in Rye. Since we had reservations, we are immediately shown to our table. Coming here brings back warmhearted memories. I remember how often we used to come here as a family on Sundays to have brunch when May and I were younger. Dad would always order Eggs Benedict.

I love Leigh and there have been many times I wished she was my biological mother. She has always loved both May and I as if we were her own biological children. Now with May away at college and my hectic work schedule, I want to get a dog to keep her company so she's not as lonely.

"I'm thinking you should have a dog at home to keep you company."

"Don't be ridiculous. I'm fine."

I scratch the back of my head. "It's not only to keep you company, but the dog can also protect you." Mom flat out refused to have hired security at the house after dad was admitted into the care facility.

She smiles kindly at me. "You're a good son, and I appreciate your concern. I'll let you get the dog if you're that worried."

"Good because I planned on doing it regardless."

"I'd like a small dog though."

I was thinking of a bigger dog like a labradoodle, or a retriever. "Sure. If that's what you want."

"Yes, it's what I want."

Our waitress comes back with our coffees, and places it down on the table.

"I heard from your father's cousin, Madeline."

I haven't heard that name in a while. Good ole cousin Maddie lives in

London, but I'm hardly close to my father's family in England. My grandfather was one of five kids, and the only one of the five who left London to attend college here in the United States. He eventually fell in love and married an American girl resulting in him staying in this country.

Dad had always been close to his cousins until he married my so-called biological mother. From what Dad had told me when I was old enough to understand, she did not take to them. One year when Madeline had come to visit, there had been a huge disagreement between Madeline and *her*. Dad never elaborated on what the disagreement was about, but Madeline was quite upset and ended up staying at a hotel instead. After that, Madeline stopped coming to the States and only spoke to my father when he was at work.

Once the divorce was final, Dad took me to visit his side of the family in England. They were all so welcoming and fun to be with. I especially enjoyed being with their kids who were close to my age.

When Madeline's husband died from a sudden heart attack, Dad flew there for the funeral. Dad's cousins from England wanted to come to Dad's funeral, but when Leigh warned them that my father's ex-wife would be there they had a change of heart. They told us it would be too difficult not to have words with her.

"How is cousin Maddie?"

"She's as well as can be. She wanted to see how we were all doing."

"That's quite kind of her to call and check on us."

"She's also planning on coming to see us in a couple of months."

"Is she really?"

"Yes. She'll be staying at the house for a couple of weeks."

I'm glad to know Mom will be busy with a houseguest. "It'll be good to see her again. Does May know?"

"Not yet. I'll let her know tonight. Madeline wants to see you. Do you think you can carve some time out of your busy schedule to see her?"

"Of course I can Mom."

"Great. Now, how is everything at work?"

"Everything is going well as it should be. I'm going back to L.A. in a few weeks, and then to Miami some time in December."

"You're always working so hard Deven. Why don't you take some time off and regroup? You haven't stopped working since Dalton's been gone."

I shake my head. "No. I don't need time off at all."

"You work much too hard."

I shrug. "Work is what I live for. What else have I got?"

"Go out and enjoy life before it's too late."

I can do that. I can also have any girl I want. Sleep with them, dump them, and move onto the next one. But it's not what I want.

"I don't have time."

"You don't have time or you don't want to make the time?" She's giving me the you-better-not-lie-to-me look.

"I don't know. Maybe a little of both?"

"We never had a chance to talk about what happened between you and Cari."

She's right. I lean back in my chair and look down at my place setting.

"What happened between you and Cari?"

"I was the one who ended it."

"You did? Why Deven?"

I rewind back to when Cari found out about my past with Lilah, and Rochelle. Then I tell her why I ended it between us.

"You handled that situation poorly. You should have told her about Lilah, and Rochelle from the beginning. How could you think she would not find out about you and Lilah when the two of them are both working in the same building?" That's her way of telling me that I'm an idiot for not picking up on that. "As for Rochelle, I never did like her much."

"I'm done with both of them."

"Good. Cari is a special girl."

"Yes, she is. She's very special. I will never find anyone like her."

"Sounds like you still care about her."

"I do."

"Have you tried to call her?"

"I did something better. I found out from Rodrigo where she worked in Boston and went to surprise her."

"That's a very impromptu thing to do. She must have been very surprised to see you."

I tell her about the reunion. The stunned look on Leigh's face does not escape me when she hears about the baby and the miscarriage.

"And now she's seeing someone."

"Oh dear."

"I'm convinced she's not over me just like I'm not over her. I want and need her back in my life. I'm nothing without her." Shaking my head I continue on. "I'm going to win her back."

She smiles at me. "I've never known you not to fight for something you really want." Neither have I.

"And she's worth fighting for."

"She is. You need to do something grand to win her back."

"I'm working on it Mom."

Our food arrives and we drop the discussion of Cari for the time being, but it does not leave my mind that I do need to show Cari how much I love her. No one will ever compare to her, and she needs to know it.

CHAPTER NINETEEN

Mid-September

CARI

The day has arrived for my two best friends to tie the knot, and I couldn't be happier for them. I returned to New York a couple of days ago to help them with the last minute preparations for their upcoming nuptials. They are scheduled to be married at City Hall this afternoon, and the reception tonight will be held at the restaurant in Central Park.

My best friends look dashing in their Armani suits. Rodrigo has on a white suit while Hunter has on a black suit. The photographer snaps some pictures of us before we get into the limo to meet up with Rodrigo's family, and Hunter's parents down at City Hall. The official ceremony is quick, and the photographer has us pose for pictures with the newlyweds in City Hall Park before we all hop into the limo and head up to Central Park for yet more pictures prior to the reception.

Being in Central Park is bittersweet especially here at Bethesda Terrace. Memories of my first date with Deven flood my mind. The rowboats on The Lake remind me of the first time he took me out on one. A warm feeling flows through me as I recall the way he looked at me with adoring eyes.

I have not heard from Deven since the day he left my apartment. I try not to think about him, but it's impossible. I can't refrain from missing him either. I hear my name being called and I turn around.

"Finally, a break! My jaw is stiff," Rodrigo says rubbing his jaw.

"Who knew taking pictures was so much work? I could never make it as a model," Hunter adds and then walks over to talk to his new brother-in-law.

Rodrigo looks at me with concern, and places his hand on my arm. "Thinking about Deven?"

He knows me so well. I shrug. "I can't help it."

"This place brings back memories doesn't it?"

"It does, but that's all they are. Just memories."

Rodrigo steers me away from everyone so we can be alone to talk.

"You miss him. I can see that you do."

What's the point in denying how I feel? "I do."

"Call him, and tell him."

"I was hoping he would have called me, but he hasn't."

"It's apparent you both are still in love with each other, but you need to make the next move. What if he changed his mind about fighting for you?"

My heart sinks at his words. Suppose he's right? I haven't heard from Deven. What if he did change his mind about fighting for me?

"Can you honestly look me in the eye and tell me that you're in love with Grady?"

"No," I say shaking my head. "It's too soon for me to be in love with him."

"Where do you see yourself with Grady?"

"I don't know."

"And the reason why you don't know is because you haven't stopped loving Deven. It's time you are honest with yourself. Spending time with Grady has been good for you, but if you can't picture yourself with him in the future, let him go so neither of you are wasting time. I hate that Deven broke your heart, but he's still in love with you."

"But I don't want him to hurt me again."

"Some men are dumb and never learn their lesson. I don't believe Deven is one of them. He knows he made a mistake when he let you go."

The photographer calls all of us back to the fountain for more pictures. Rodrigo takes my hands. "Don't wait too long and give him the opportunity to get away. Not too many people get a second chance to start over. You two are meant to be." He gestures his head to the fountain. "Let's get back for more pictures."

The entire restaurant is closed to the public to accommodate Rodrigo and

Hunter's reception. The restaurant has been transformed into something truly magical. Tulle and fairy lights suspend from the ceiling while tall floral centerpieces with dangling crystals sit on each table giving the entire space an enchanting look.

"Cari?"

I turn around to see who called my name and see Alana. "Alana!" We hug each other.

"It's so good to see you."

Alana and I chat every day, but I have not seen her in a while as she's been tasked to help out in Los Angeles.

"And you as well. Where's V?"

"He's getting me a ginger ale." A ginger ale? I stare at her. Can it be? Is she pregnant? She looks like she gained some weight.

"I have very good news to share with you."

"What is it?"

"We're having a baby!"

Though I suspected she is pregnant, my heart aches at the news. I am happy for her, but I also can't help feel sad that she's pregnant and I'm not.

"That's great. Congratulations." I force a smile on my face. "How far along are you?"

"I'm three months." She's glowing with happiness. "How are things with Grady?"

I never made mention to her about Deven's presence in Boston, but now seems to be the perfect time to bring it up. "Things with Grady are good, but I saw Deven."

"He's here?"

"No. He was in Boston."

"I knew he was in Boston, but I didn't know he was in touch with you."

"He wasn't. He was meeting up with friends at the hotel's bar, and he happened to see me." I fill her in on the rest of the encounter.

"Cari, I told you he's been miserable without you. There's no doubt in my mind he that he still loves you. I didn't want to say anything to you because I wanted you to be happy and get on with your life, but when I mentioned to

Deven a while back that you had moved on he was visibly upset. He acted like he didn't care, but clearly he did and still does. He's always worked hard, but when he had you he took time to enjoy his personal life. Ever since Dalton died, Deven's just poured himself back into work again and he's been moody."

"Alana, I don't know who to choose."

She puts her hand on my arm. "Trust your heart."

I nod and she changes the subject back to her pregnancy until Vinny returns with her ginger ale. Vinny seems genuinely concerned about Alana being on her feet and takes her over to their table. I tell them I will be there shortly.

There's a longing in my heart as I watch my two best friends dance. They're so happy and so in love, and it makes me realize I do want a happy ever after with Deven. He made me whole again, and put so much joy in my heart. Even after my heart shattered into a million pieces, I never stopped loving him and I know I never will.

I was given the honor to be both the maid-of-honor, and the best man at their wedding. When it's time to make the speech, the emcee introduces me and hands over the microphone. I quickly down the rest of my wine and nervously take the microphone to deliver my speech. I had written everything down on a small sheet of paper, but find that I do not need to refer to it once I start to speak. The memories are all in my head and my heart and the words flow naturally.

I am so happy to have been a part of Rodrigo and Hunter's special day. Being in love is truly an amazing thing. I know this because I was once very much in love with the most incredible guy I had ever met. And I hope to be able to experience such love again.

CHAPTER TWENTY

CARI

I lay the large bouquet of flowers down on the freshly cut grass and lean a small teddy bear against the tombstone. My eyes scan the three names inscribed on it. All of them gone too soon. Soon the fourth name will be added on. I sit down on the grass wrapping my arms around my knees as I cry for the loss of my baby. It's been said time heals all wounds, but I disagree. The pain of losing the baby has not gotten any easier and I wonder if it ever will be.

My mind is occupied with the memories I have of Deven and I. When I graduated college, I envisioned myself working hard to climb the ladder of success. Instead, I fell in love with swoon worthy and charismatic Deven Blake, and became pregnant with his baby. The baby that is now gone.

The past couple of nights have been sleepless ones. I had done nothing but toss and turn thinking about Deven and Grady. Both are wonderful men, and the thought of having to hurt either one of them pains me. Life isn't always fair, and I have to make a choice. I hope I don't regret the choice I am about to make.

A couple of hours later, I get off at the Columbus Circle station and walk over to BG headquarters. It's a little after five and people are leaving work.

"Miss Snow?"

I take my gaze off of the building and see Jimmy the security guard outside.

"Hi Jimmy."

He shakes my hand. "Miss Snow. How good it is to see you back here."

"It's good to see you too Jimmy. How have you been?"

"As well as can be. And yourself?"

"I've been good."

"Are you coming back?"

Sadly, I shake my head.

"That's too bad. You were the sunshine of this place."

"Thank you. How is your family?"

"They're all good. Elisa is going to start college soon." Elisa is his youngest daughter.

"How wonderful. Which college will she be attending?"

"Iona College. She wanted to stay close to home."

"It's a wonderful school. Congratulations to her."

"Thank you Miss Snow."

I look at the time on my watch. "Do you know if Deven is still here?"

"I believe he is. Come with me. I'll let you up."

I follow Jimmy into the building, and he allows me to bypass the security checkpoint. We chat all the way to the elevator bank and I thank him again for letting me up to the offices. When I get off the elevator I notice the office has pretty much cleared out except for a few faces I do not recognize. I walk over to Myra's department, but it looks like everyone has gone home for the day. Maybe Myra was in a good mood today and let everyone go home early Alana has left for the day as well. I stroll through the office and before I know it, I am over by Catrina's desk. Catrina's face registers shock when she sees me.

"Oh my God! Cari?"

I give her a nod and she comes around her desk to hug me.

"It's great seeing you again," I say.

"You too. How are you?"

"Not too bad. What about you?"

"Good. Can't complain."

We're making small talk when I notice Deven's windows are opaque. Is someone in there with him? I gather my nerves together and ask her if Deven is still in his office.

"He is. I'll let him know you're here."

"No. I want to surprise him."

"Oh! He'll be very surprised then!"

"The other side of the office is practically empty. Why are you still here?"

"I have to make sure Deven has all the papers he needs for tomorrow's trip so I'm in the midst of collating all of it." I'm ever so glad I made the decision to come today. Tomorrow would have been too late. "Let me buzz him." She rounds her desk and calls him using the speakerphone.

"Yes, Cat?"

The sound of Deven's voice makes my heart race.

"You need to sign off on some proposals. Can I come in and have you sign them before you leave?"

"You may come in," Deven says before hanging up.

She presses the speakerphone button to hang up. "I'll be leaving soon so I'll let you two catch up."

"Thanks."

"Don't mention it." She hugs me again. "Stop by again."

I take a deep breath to try to help me relax. *We're meant to be.* I open his door and step inside. He is immersed in paperwork, and does not bother to look up. I nervously clear my throat to get his attention. He raises his head, and his mouth drops open. He immediately stands up, removes his glasses, and comes towards me.

"Cari."

"Hi."

"What a very delightful surprise."

I push my hair back behind my ear, and offer a smile.

"What brings you to New York?"

"Oh. I, um…" I look towards the ceiling before continuing, "I came back for Rodrigo and Hunter's wedding. They got married on Friday."

His eyes widen in surprise. "That's wonderful news. Please give them my congratulations."

"I'll be sure to pass along your message."

"Were you in the neighborhood?"

I bite on my lower lip hoping I made the right decision. I need to be strong and go through with this. I throw my arms around his neck, but he doesn't respond like I was anticipating. He doesn't wrap his arms around me right away and I begin to think I made the wrong decision. As I start to peel away, I feel his strong muscular arms hook around my waist and he holds me tightly to him. He clings to me like he is holding on for his life. I lay my head on his shoulder. He strokes my hair as we stand there savoring the moment, not wanting to let the other go. When we finally do pull apart, Deven tilts my chin up and locks his eyes with mine.

He cradles one of my cheeks in his hand and strokes it with his thumb. "Angel, I'm so elated right now."

I want to laugh, and cry, and kiss him madly. I lean into his hand. Oh how I've missed his touch.

"I am too," I say as he reaches for my hand and brings it up to his lips to plant a kiss on it.

"Does this mean it's over between you and Grady?"

I close my eyes briefly and shake my head. "I haven't told him yet."

"Oh." He purses his lips.

"I will tell him, but it brings me no pleasure to have to hurt him."

"I know." He pulls me back to him and runs his hands up and down my back. "I'm just so happy to have you back in my life." He presses a kiss to the top of my head. "And I'm never letting you go again."

Pressing my cheek against his chest, I let out a content sigh. The broken pieces of my heart are slowly fitting back together. I don't want him to ever let me go again.

CHAPTER TWENTY-ONE

DEVEN

She's here. I am over the fucking moon with happiness. I have been devising a plan to win her back, and here she stands before me. *She came to me.* After what I did to her I am not worthy of a second chance, but I'm thankful that I am getting one. And I'll be damned if I let her go again.

"Cari, you're everything to me. I love you very much," I tell her as I look into her beautiful jade eyes.

"I love you very much as well."

Hearing her say those words back to me pleases me to no end. I want to hear say that to me forever. I will never tire of hearing her say it.

"Why don't we go have dinner and talk?"

"I'd like that."

I kiss her forehead. "Let me just get my stuff together and we can leave."

I close the files I have open on my desk and stack them neatly in place. I check to make sure I have everything I need. Taking her hand I lead her out of my office. It feels good to hold her hand once again. As we wait for the elevator, a few of my new employees join us and make small talk to me as they take notice of our clasped hands. One of the girls can't seem to stop staring at me and it causes Cari to grip my hand tighter. I let everyone off first when we reach the lobby.

"How about we go have your favorite? Thai food?"

"You remember."

"Cari, I remember everything about you."

I take her to the new Thai restaurant several blocks away from the office. We are seated, and a few minutes later our waiter comes by to take our orders.

"Angel, I can't tell you how fucking ecstatic I am right now. I was planning on going back to Boston for you."

"You really were?"

"Without question. I had something grand in mind to win you back, but you beat me to it. I'm so glad you did, and that you're mine again."

"Deven, I need to break it off with Grady first."

I let out a sigh. *Like I need the reminder.* "Yeah, I guess you do."

She looks down at her place setting.

"How is your friend Zach?" I have to start learning to accept that he is nothing more than a friend to her.

"He's good. There was never anything going on between Zach and I. He's always known how I felt about you. He's been nothing more than a friend, and friends don't come easy to me. He will always be a friend to me."

It's all about trust, and I need to trust her. I do trust her. I just need to trust him. "I know. You did tell this to me. And besides, you wouldn't be with what's his name if you were with Zach."

"His name is Grady." I really don't care what his name is. "I moved on because I thought you had moved on with Rochelle. Losing you was hard, but losing the baby was even harder. The baby was the only thing I had left of you. It seemed so final."

I place my hand over hers and give it a squeeze. "It wasn't final. We're together again." I stroke her thumb with mine.

"There's something I need to tell you."

"What is it?" I ask anxiously.

"The day of your father's funeral, I had wanted to speak to you, but your mother…" She trails off and I know why. I'll make it easy for her.

"I don't consider her to be my mother, but I am aware of what she did to you."

"You are? How?"

I hurry and explain how I came to learn of this. Cari then tells me about the exchange between her and *that woman.* Listening to her recount what was said to her infuriates me. I offer an apology, but she astonishes me when she tells me it's *that woman* who should be the one apologizing. And she cannot be more right. That bitch owes my girl a huge apology.

Cari transitions the conversation to Hunter and Rodrigo's wedding. I wish I could have been there as well, but I understand why an invitation was not extended to me. After dinner, we walk together to the parking garage where my Maserati is. I prefer she comes back home with me, but she will probably not do so as long as she is still technically with Grady. How I hate that name. I can't wait until she ends it with him. As we near the apartment, the eurphoic feeling I have is dissipating. I don't want this night to end yet.

"Why don't we go for coffee?" I catch her smiling. "Why are you smiling?"

"It brought back the memory of the first time we went to the coffee shop together."

I can't help but smile as well. "I didn't want that night to end."

"Nor did I."

"And I don't want tonight to end yet. Join me for coffee?"

She gives me a nod. I park the car several blocks away from the coffee shop, and we stroll down the street hand in hand. Being here with her again is fucking sensational, but a disturbing thought has been nagging me about her and Grady.

"I have to ask you something."

"Sure. What is it?"

"Have you slept with Grady?"

She stops her pace and looks up at me. Her eyes seem darker. Shit. She's furious. I should have kept my mouth shut. Screwing this up now is not a good idea.

"No. I did not."

A wave of relief washes over me. I pull her to me and kiss her not caring that we're on the sidewalk with many onlookers. "When do you leave to go back to Boston?"

"Tomorrow."

"I'm going back with you."

"That's not necessary."

"It isn't an option."

"But you have your trip to L.A. tomorrow."

"I can cancel and go later."

She shakes her head and puts her palm up against my chest. "It's best if I go back myself and break it gently to Grady."

The thought of not being there with her is not sitting well with me. "I don't need to be there with you when you tell him, but I don't want to be apart from you. We've already been away from each other for too long. Please Cari."

"All right Deven."

I place a kiss on her forehead before we continue our stroll to the coffee shop. Once we are seated, the waiter comes over immediately to take our orders. The service here is impeccable.

"How has your search for an assistant been?"

"I have an assistant at last."

"Oh, that's great Deven."

"He is great, and has the potential to move up in the company."

"He?"

"Yep. He's probably around your age, and working to pay his way through college." I tell her all about him and how overjoyed I was to get rid of the temp.

After coffee, I escort her back to the apartment trying to find reasons to stay with her a little longer, but I fail to come up with one.

"What time shall I be here tomorrow?"

She tilts her head to the side. "Why do you have to leave at all?"

~ * ~

CARI

Deven appears to be surprised by my question. I want him to stay with me tonight. We've been separated long enough, and my body is throbbing for him. It's not my intention to hurt Grady, but in my heart it's always been Deven. Deven is the reason why I held myself back from further advancing my relationship with Grady. And the thought of sleeping with Grady has never even entered my mind.

Deven takes another step closer, cradles my face, and gently kisses me. The kiss quickly becomes passionate…neither of us can get enough of the other. He finally pulls back and looks deep into my eyes.

"Come back home with me tonight."

Still breathless from the kiss, I nod to indicate that I will go back with him. We make our way up to Hunter and Rodrigo's apartment. Once inside, he closes the door and draws me to him for another deep kiss. When we break from the kiss, I go into my room and pack my bag. He brings my bag to the car and drives us back to his penthouse.

When I step out of his car at the building, I am greeted with a huge smile by the valet.

"It's nice to see you again Cari."

"And it's nice to see you again too Roger."

"Are you back for good?" he asks me softly as Deven collects my bag from the trunk.

"Yes," I whisper back.

He gives me another smile right as Deven stands beside me.

"Keys are in the car. Have a good night Roger."

"And a good night to both of you as well."

Deven grabs my hand leading us into the building and directly to the elevator. We ride up to his floor, and he opens the door for me.

"Welcome home." He closes the door, sets the alarm, and places a kiss on my cheek. "Let me put your bag down in our room."

Our room. I follow him to the master room. He places my bag in his ginormous walk-in closet and pulls me to him. My cheek rests comfortably against his chest.

"I haven't been home much after our separation." He kisses the top of my head and releases me. His hands frame my face and he looks at me affectionately.

"I am never letting you go again. I am nothing without you. This time it will be for keeps. I promise." His lips meet mine and he gives me an earth shattering kiss. I will never get tired of kissing him.

After unpacking my bag, I sit on the bed flipping through a book while Deven finishes up some work. I look over at the other nightstand and see that he still has the picture of us from Alana's wedding. We were very happy then, and very much in love. We still are. I close my eyes and pray silently that we will make it work this time.

A call comes through on my phone. Uh-oh. It's Grady. I ignore the call and shut off my phone. I am not ready to speak to him, and will have to deal with him tomorrow. But what will happen after that? Do I stay in Boston or do I come back to New York? It's a decision I cannot make alone. I get out of bed and join Deven in his office. He looks up at me and removes his glasses.

"Hey gorgeous. Everything okay?"

"Yeah. I was just thinking about us."

"Come here."

I go over to him and he pulls me down onto his lap. He pushes my hair to the side and nuzzles his mouth to my neck.

"Tell me exactly what you were thinking about."

"I left New York to start over in Boston. You're here and I'm there."

"And you're thinking one of us should move."

"One of us will have to."

He rubs my arm. "If you're happy in Boston, I will not hesitate to move. We can keep the penthouse and come back on the weekends. I can remotely work anywhere in the world, but I absolutely refuse for us to be apart again. We'll continue this discussion in the morning. It's late, and I'm done here. Let's go to bed."

I slide off his lap and something in the corner of his desk catches my attention. It's a picture of a little girl with curly blonde locks. She has blonde hair like Rochelle. Panic starts to set in, and I gasp. Does he have a daughter with her?

"That's my niece." His niece? "Ken's daughter."

"Ken has a daughter?"

"Yeah." He tells me how Ken found out about his daughter, and I am filled with even more remorse for keeping the news about our baby from Deven. He would have taken care of me, and the baby. Our child would never be deprived of love. We would have been doting parents.

"Hey." He looks into my teary eyes. "You're thinking about our baby." How does he always know what's on my mind?

A traitor tear escapes and rolls down my cheek. He wipes it away with his finger.

"There'll be another baby someday." I look at him. He's promising me another baby. My heart is singing with joy. I want another baby with him. I do.

He kisses my eyes, nose, and then my lips. Lips still connected, he scoops me into his arms and carries me into the bedroom. He sets me down on the bed, and quickly unbuttons his shirt in record time. He takes it off and reaches for the bottom of his t-shirt. I put my hands over his to stop him. I lift the bottom of his shirt and pull it off of him. My fingers gingerly trace each hard rippling muscle on his chest. God, he's gorgeous. And he's mine. *All mine.*

CHAPTER TWENTY-TWO

CARI

Waking up in Deven's muscular arms is heavenly. And reconciliation sex is extremely heavenly. The way he touched me and then…well, one can use their creative mind as to what happened between him and me. I'm thrilled to be with him again. I turn my head back and stare at the magnificent man lying beside me. His hair is disheveled and he looks so cute asleep. I stretch my arm and reach for my phone on the nightstand. I turn it on and see there are ten missed calls from Grady. I close my eyes hating the fact that I have to hurt him. I type a quick response letting him know I will return to Boston later in the day and asked if we can meet up then. I place the phone back down on the nightstand, and turn back over to Deven. I gently tuck his hair behind his ear. He opens those striking blue eyes I love so much, and a smile spreads across his face.

"Good morning angel."

"Good morning."

"I missed having you beside me in bed." He lays a hand on my cheek. "You'll never know how sorry I am for hurting you."

"I should have trusted you."

"I gave you reason not to trust me, but it will not happen again. Being apart from you nearly killed me angel."

I pull his hand off of my cheek and thread my fingers with his. "I don't ever want to be apart from you again."

"Never." He places three kisses on my lips. "What time do you plan to leave for Boston?"

"I was thinking about eleven."

"The sooner the better."

It's apparent he wants me to finish it with Grady as soon as we return which I plan on doing, but it does not give me any kind of joy to break his heart. "We have some time before we have to leave. Why don't we make good use of it?" I decide to be bold and do something I have never dared to do. I let my hand travel down to his manhood. I stroke it and watch his face take pleasure in what I am doing to him.

"Cari." He struggles to say my name in between breaths. "What you do to me..."

I roll him onto his back and straddle him. I raise myself and slowly sink down over him. I toss my head back and...oh. *Oh God. Feels so good.* I move up and down watching him as he becomes undone. Together we move in perfect harmony until we both reach that point. Then I look back down at him and stare into his spellbinding blue eyes. I am so in love with this extraordinary man, and I will do whatever I have to in order to hold onto him. He's so worth it.

~ * ~

Deven brings our bags into my apartment placing them in the bedroom first.

"It's almost time for you to meet Brady."

"It's Grady."

I made plans to meet Grady this afternoon. We hit so much traffic on the trip here that I hardly have much time to freshen up.

"I think I'll go in with you."

I shake my head. "No. I think it's best if I go in alone. Please."

His jaw clenches. "I'll wait for you somewhere nearby then."

"It's what we agreed to isn't it?"

He doesn't want me to do this alone, but I have to. It kills me that I have to hurt Grady. He deserves so much better.

I arrive a few minutes late and find Grady sitting at a table staring at his phone. His face breaks into a smile when he sees me. He immediately approaches me and enfolds me in his arms. Then he moves to kiss me, but I turn my face slightly to avoid the kiss.

"I'm so glad you're back. I missed you."

All I can offer is a smile in return. I can't get myself to say the words back to him. Can he sense how uncomfortable I am right now? He pulls out my seat for me, and I thank him as I lower myself into the chair.

"What would you like me to get you? A cappuccino?"

I shake my head.

"Is everything okay Cari? Did something happen while you were in New York?"

Yes, something did happen, and I need to just tell him.

"I...I don't know how to tell you..."

"Tell me what?"

"These past couple of months with you has been really great. You're such a sweet guy, but -"

He stops me from continuing. "No need to say anymore. I think I get what you're trying to say."

I can see the hurt in his eyes. "I'm so sorry."

He shakes his head. "I do want to ask you something."

"Of course."

"Is it him? Are you back with your ex-boyfriend?"

I give him a nod.

"I guessed that much. I don't think this is fair to me. I never got a fair chance to show you that I can make you happy."

His statement is accurate. I should not have agreed to go out with him in the first place. My heart belongs to Deven. It always has and it always will.

"I'm so sorry."

He shakes his head. "No hard feelings, all right? I really wish you all the best." He stands up and stops next to me. "Be happy Cari." He leans down and places a kiss on my forehead before walking away.

I don't know how long I stay seated in the chair with my hands over my mouth. It's not my nature to hurt people. I feel a warm hand press against my back.

"Hey."

Deven had been waiting across the street while I spoke to Grady. I can't bring myself to look at him right this moment as he sits down in the chair that Grady had sat in. He gently peels my hands away from my mouth and holds them in between his.

"You okay?"

I draw in a deep breath and let it out before answering. "That was so very hard to do."

"But it had to be done." He brings one of my hands to his lips and places a kiss on it. "I love you, and I promise we're in this together for the long run."

I close my eyes. "That's all I want." When I open my eyes I find his brilliant blue eyes gazing back at me. He takes one of his hands and lays it on my cheek. I lean into it. It may be over with Grady, but I have a new beginning with Deven.

CHAPTER TWENTY-THREE

CARI

Deven and I have been discussing our future living arrangements. He left the final decision of our residence to me. He is willing to relocate if I choose Boston, but the reason why I moved to Boston in the first place was to be away from him. I didn't want to leave New York, but at the time it hurt too much to be so near him. If I choose New York, he expects me to move in with him. Hunter and Rodrigo will not object to my living with them if I decide to move back to Manhattan, but they are married now and I need to respect their privacy. I know exactly what I want and what I want is to be with Deven.

The movers that Deven hired arrived bright and early this morning while I was still in bed. Deven had returned to New York this past week to take care of business matters, but he is on his way back and should arrive within the next couple of hours. He offered to help me pack even though I insisted it was not necessary. The ring coming from my cell phone interrupts me from packing and I go to grab it off the nightstand.

"Hello?"

"Angel, you sound exhausted."

"That's because I am. The movers showed up at seven."

"Goddamn them. I told them not to get there before eight."

"It's okay. I had to get up anyway."

"It's really not okay. I am paying these people to show up on time, not an hour early." Deven is a stickler on being prompt.

"Deven, leave it alone."

He sighs. "Fine. I just passed Essex, and should be there in a couple of hours."

"Get here soon."

"I will. I love you Cari."

"I love you too Deven."

I return to packing some of the smaller items that are on the shelf. I have already packed five small boxes when the doorbell rings. I check the time. It can't be Deven unless he was lying about where he was when I spoke to him. I shake that ridiculous thought out of my head. No, he wouldn't do that to me. Who can it be at this hour of the morning? I open the door surprised to find Grady standing there with his hands in his pockets.

"Hi Cari."

"Hi."

"I'm sorry for the early intrusion. I heard you're leaving Boston."

Oh. Faith must have told him. I push some strands of loose hair behind my ear.

"Yes, I am. I will be leaving tomorrow morning, but my furniture and the bulky items go today."

"I'm glad I got here in time to say goodbye."

Wow. What a remarkable guy he is for coming here to wish me farewell after I broke his heart. He deserves someone so much better than me.

"That's really sweet of you to stop by. You could have called so you didn't have to make a trip here."

He shrugs. "I think it's better to say goodbye in person." He stares down at the floor. "You're very special, and I hope I can meet someone else like you."

I place a hand on his arm. "You'll meet someone better."

He shakes his head. "Someone better than you? I don't think that's possible. I hope your boyfriend realizes how fortunate he is to have you."

Deven does realize it, and I am just as fortunate to have him. I will never love anyone else.

"Would you like to come in? Unfortunately, I can't make you any coffee. The machine has been packed away."

"Thank you, but I have to get going. Good luck with everything."

I instinctively hug him. "Take care of yourself Grady."

"You do the same Cari," he says as he hugs me a little tighter. "If you ever need anything you have my number."

"I do. Thanks."

He waves before leaving, and I silently pray he will find the girl of his dreams someday.

CHAPTER TWENTY-FOUR

CARI

Staying at home and waiting for Deven to return from work is a humdrum experience. I want to work again and focus on building my career. Deven prefers I return to work at BG, but I cannot bring myself to go back there and face his employees after what we have been through. I will not be able to handle the whispering behind my back.

While I have been home, I try my hand at redesigning his company's website. When I finished my project, I show him the samples I created. He leans in closer to me.

"These are phenomenal. I want this to be the company's new website," he says as he points to the sample he likes best.

"You do?"

"Yes, I do angel." He gives me a kiss on my cheek.

"It still needs improvement."

He lifts my chin. "No, it does not. This is excellent. I really want to use this as the company's website." He pushes my hair away and plants kisses on my neck. *Mmmm.*

"So, uh, does this mean I'm hired?"

"Definitely angel."

"I'll be working for you again?"

"Do you object?"

"No, but I prefer if I do not have to go into the office."

"Why?"

"I'm not ready to face everyone after what happened between us. People will be whispering."

"Does it really matter what they say or even think?"

"Yes."

"I'll fire anyone who makes you feel uncomfortable."

Oh no, I can't allow that to happen.

"We'll compromise. Why don't you work from home for the time being?"

"Really? I can?"

"Of course angel. However, I will need you to come into the office from time to time."

I swallow, and then shake my head.

"You need not pay those gossipmongers any attention."

I can't disregard what people will think of me.

"What others say or think should not matter at all. Just focus on your work."

I nod. I will do that. I will concentrate on my job. "Do we have a deal then?"

He tilts his head to the side. "Why don't we seal the deal in bed?"

"Is that how you seal all of your deals?"

His lips curl into a smile. "Only with you angel."

~ * ~

DEVEN

Today Cari has brought me to the cemetery where our baby is interred with her mother, and her grandparents. I would have preferred if our baby rested alongside my father, but I wasn't in the picture when the decision was being made. Cari kneels down in front of the tombstone. A wave of emotion sweeps over me as I watch her place the bouquets of flowers into the in-ground vases. She carefully arranges the flowers, and then bows her head.

I choke back down a sob, and kneel down next to her. I seem to be at a loss for words. What do I say? I close my eyes and say a silent prayer. I stand first and help her to her feet. Tears are streaming down her face. I pull her into my arms and hold her as we grieve together for the child we lost. I wipe away my tears first, and then gently wipe away hers with my thumbs.

"Oh Deven. If only the baby survived."

I shush her and frame her beautiful face in my hands. "The baby is in a better place. Someday there will be another baby." And there will be.

I kiss her forehead and take her hand leading her back to the car where Mauricio is waiting for us. After I strap my seatbelt on, I place her hands between mine.

"It must have been so hard for you to have dealt with the loss on your own." I lift her hand and drop a kiss on it.

"It was. *It still is hard.*" She closes her eyes briefly and continues. "I'm so thankful Rodrigo was with me that day. If he hadn't called the ambulance…"

My heart leaps at the word *ambulance*. "What exactly happened that day?"

She lays her head on my shoulder and tells me. Listening to her and the devastation in her voice kills me. I didn't realize the depth of her anguish. Losing the baby is upsetting, but I am extremely grateful she survived.

"Deven?"

"Yes?"

"What would you have done if I had told you I was pregnant?"

I pull back so I can look into her gorgeous eyes. "I would have begged for your forgiveness first. Then I would have married you and taken care of you and the baby. We would become a family."

"Will you forgive me for not telling you?" She looks at me imploringly.

"There's nothing to forgive. I understand why you kept it from me." I lean forward and place a tender kiss on her lips. "I love you Carilyn. I always will. You're the only one for me."

CHAPTER TWENTY-FIVE

Mid-October

DEVEN

My long hours at work have been reduced since I've reunited with Cari. I intend to spend as much time as I can with her to make up for our time apart. Two weeks ago, I surprised her with the news that I would be whisking her away for an entire week. We're now on our way to a private island I have rented, and am considering purchasing.

My private plane starts to circle the island as it prepares to land. Cari looks out the window and immediately her pretty mouth opens wide.

"That's all ours for the week?"

"Yes, it is. Only the staff will be there besides us." What she doesn't know is that I have given the staff specific instructions on when to be visible.

"This is…" She trails off transfixed by the sight of the island.

"Going to be one of the best weeks we've had in months," I say finishing her sentence.

My pilot announces that he is preparing to land and we buckle up. A car is ready to drive us back to the house once we exit the plane. As soon as the plane is parked on the runway, the stewardess gets up from her seat to open the door and set up the air stairs for our disembarkment.

"Are you ready?" I ask as I unbuckle my seatbelt.

"I'm ready."

We rise from our seats, gather our belongings, and leave the aircraft. I grab her hand and lead her towards my new Rolls Royce Phantom.

She peers up at me. "Whoa! Is that what I think it is?"

I nod proudly.

"Good day Mr. Blake, and Miss Snow." That's Jordan. He's the new chauffeur and bodyguard I hired for us. Mauricio will continue to serve as our primary chauffeur in New York while Jordan will start to accompany us when we leave this island.

"Who is he?" she asks once he shuts her door.

"His name is Jordan. He's our new driver, and also doubles as our personal security detail."

"We need security?"

I kiss the top of her hand. "Yes, angel we do." Keeping her safe is one of my top priorities.

She turns to look out the window as we begin the journey to the house. I point out the beach to her along the way. There's nothing but miles and miles of white sand surrounding this island. Jordan stops in front of the house. He comes around and opens the door for Cari to step out.

"Wow! This really is ours for the week?" she asks again as she looks around.

"It is. It's going to be just the two of us for the entire week."

The front door opens. "Welcome Mr. Blake, and Miss Snow." That's the butler.

"Thank you Wyeth." I step aside to let Cari in first.

"They all know who I am," she whispers.

"They're supposed to. Get used to it," I whisper back as I hold her hand.

She shakes her head as I show her around the two level, eight bedroom art deco house we will be staying in. I bring her to our room which has a view of the ocean as well as the infinity pool.

"This is so amazing!"

I knew she would love this. She takes my face in her hands and kisses me. I make a mental note to surprise her much more often.

"I'm glad you like it."

"Like it? I love it!"

I take her hands and gaze deeply into her eyes. "I screwed up our relationship, and I want to make up for it and all the time we lost. I promise not to make the same mistake again. I want you to trust me again Cari."

"I do trust you Deven."

My heart swells at her words. That's all I need to hear. I will never do anything to lose her trust in me again.

CHAPTER TWENTY-SIX

CARI

The past week has been nothing but delightful. Tonight's dinner will be served in the courtyard which is surrounded by lush tropical flowers and plants. Tiki lanterns circle the courtyard and steel drum music streams through hidden speakers.

Deven pulls out the chair for me and kisses the top of my head once I am seated. An elaborate candelabrum sits in the center of the table between us. He opens the bottle of wine that is chilling in the bucket and pours some into our glasses.

"I need to speak to you about something important that's been on my mind."

Oh. What can it be?

"I want you to take on a more prominent role with BG."

"Such as?"

"I want you to become my adviser."

I stare back at him incredulously not sure if I heard him correctly. "Your adviser?"

"Yes. I want you to be my adviser on future acquisitions and new projects."

I barely have any knowledge of real estate development and acquisitions. How can he want my input on things I am not familiar with?

"I don't understand."

"What don't you understand?"

"You have a team in place, and I hardly know much about acquisitions. Why would you want to consult with me?"

He reaches for my hand across the table. "Because I trust you and value your advice. I want you to become more involved in the real estate world. I want for us to be a team. Most of all, I despise not being with you all day long."

"But my career –"

"I don't want you to give up your dream, but you also have talent for this trade. I've seen your work. I've heard your ideas in meetings. You're perfect for the position."

I am extremely flattered he thinks I am. "You think so?"

"I know so." He cups my face with his hand. "I don't need an answer now. Take some time and think about it, okay?"

"I promise I will." A career in real estate for me? Is this something I want to pursue? It's definitely something I really need to think through.

After we finish with dessert, he suggests we take a walk on the beach and watch the sunset. What a perfect night it is to do so. The sunset combined with the pristine white sand and lucid turquoise water is magnificent. We remove our sandals and let our feet sink in the sand. He laces his fingers with mine and leans into me for a long deep kiss.

I wish we didn't have to leave tomorrow. As we continue our leisurely walk, I notice something illuminating the beach up ahead. It's not until we get closer does everything come into focus. *Oh wow!* There has to be hundreds of candles scattered throughout the sand. I've never seen anything like it. It's so romantic.

"I have a surprise for you."

"You do?"

"Cover your eyes with your other hand."

I do as he requests, and he pulls me with him. What kind of surprise does he have planned for me now?

"Open your eyes angel," he says when he comes to a stop.

I let my hand drop and open my eyes. I gasp. There are candles in the sand formed in the shape of a heart. Etched in the sand inside the heart are our initials:

CJS

+

DAB

I peer up at Deven. "Oh my. No one has ever done anything like this for me. I must take a picture of it." He lets out a soft laugh as he shakes his head. I snap a couple of pictures with my phone, and turn back around to find Deven on one knee holding open a box containing a huge diamond in it. My hand immediately flies over my mouth, and my eyes start to dampen.

"Cari, from the moment I laid eyes on you I knew I had to have you. I didn't think true love existed until you came into my life. I want my days to begin and end with you. I want to wake up in the morning and go to sleep at night with you right beside me. I want to spend the rest of my life loving you, protecting you, and taking care of you. I want to have a lot of babies with you. You deserve your happy ever after and I want to be the one to give it to you. Be my wife, my lifetime lover and partner, and the mother of my children. Carilyn Jade Snow, I hope you will do me the honor and say yes to becoming Mrs. Deven Blake."

Oh. My. God. Tears flow endlessly from my eyes. I can't believe this is happening to me. I'm elated. I have my prince and he wants to give me my happy ever after. I wipe away my tears and gaze into his own watery eyes.

"Yes! I will be honored to become Mrs. Deven Blake."

A wide smile appears on his face, and he pulls the ring out of the box. He takes my left hand and manages to slide it onto my finger despite my trembling hand. He kisses my hand and stands up. Framing my face with his hands, he kisses me slowly and deeply until we both have to pull back for air.

"I love you so very much Cari. I can't imagine going through the rest of my life without you by my side."

My eyes tear up again at his admission because that's exactly how I feel. "I feel the same."

He holds my hand up and admires the sparkling diamond ring. I can't help but admire it as well. The three-carat cushion cut ring has diamonds framing it with smaller diamonds set around the platinum band. It is absolutely stunning. The most beautiful ring I have ever seen. "This ring is gorgeous!"

"I'm glad you think so. I had it custom designed exclusively for you. I had it made for you before Christmas of last year and was planning to give it to you, but things didn't go as I had planned."

His revelation stuns me. "You knew that early?"

He smiles showing off his dimples. "Yeah, I did. I fell head over heels for you. Close your eyes. I have another surprise for you." Another surprise? With my hand in his, he tugs me along.

When he tells me to open my eyes, I am bowled over at what I see. Before me is a canopied bed with rose petals scattered on the bedcover. How did he manage to get a bed on the beach? *Sheesh!* Flameless candles and lanterns circle the bed, and there's a bottle of chilled champagne waiting for us.

"Let's celebrate our engagement." He pops open the champagne and pours it into two flutes. He places the bottle back in the ice bucket and hands me a flute before taking his. "To us Cari, and our new beginning."

Our glasses touch and we take a drink. He takes our glasses and sets it on the small round table next to the bed. Turning back to me he places his hands on my neck and kisses me relishing my lips. *Mmmm.* His hands slide down my back and work to unzip my dress. The strapless dress falls to the ground. His fingers delicately caress the back of my neck and work its way down to my breasts before stopping at my waist. I lie down on the bed and watch as he swiftly removes his clothes to join me.

"Thank you." He kisses the tip of my nose

I stare into his dreamy azure eyes. "I don't understand what you're thanking me for."

"For giving me another chance and for agreeing to marry me."

"Oh Deven. There's no one else but you."

"And there's no one else for me but you."

"Together."

"Forever baby."

He kisses me and his tongue slowly makes the journey down to…oh… mmmm-hmmm…well, you get the idea.

CHAPTER TWENTY-SEVEN

DEVEN

I prop my head up and look at my gorgeous fiancée lying in bed next to me. I am the luckiest and happiest guy in the world. She said *yes*. If I had my way I would marry her today, but she deserves to have the wedding of her dreams. I stroke her cheek and her eyes flutter open. Beautiful.

"Good morning my beautiful angel."

She smiles at me. "Good morning."

"How did you sleep?"

"Well. How could I not after last night?"

She's right. Celebratory mind-blowing sex is fucking fabulous. We went at it quite a few times until we finally became exhausted.

"We can have a repeat of last night."

"I'm all for it, but first I want to share our happy news with Rodrigo and Hunter."

I suppose I should inform my family, and Brad as well.

"We'll let our families know first, and then officially announce it on social media." I want the entire world to know about our engagement. Her smile fades. Not a good sign. "What's wrong?"

"I was hoping we can keep it to just the family for now."

"Why?"

"I'm not ready to announce it to the public yet. There's going to be a lot of women out there who will be very disappointed to learn you're no longer available."

The only thing that is disappointing here is the request to keep our happy news a damn secret. Why can't she see that?

"Angel, why does it matter if those women are disappointed?"

"They're going to hate me."

"You can't please everyone sweetheart."

"It's only for a little while."

I lean back against my pillow and give in. "Alright. For now, it will be only our family who will know about our engagement. We do have the gala in a couple of weeks, and I want to introduce you as my fiancée." This gala we are going to means a lot to me as it benefits research for Alzheimer's. I am one of the donors and it pleases me immensely that Cari will be attending the event with me.

She kisses my cheek. "Thank you."

"Guess we should go back to the house and wash up."

We both get up and I pick up our clothes. I shake out the sand and hand Cari her dress before shaking out the sand from my clothes and putting them back on. We walk back to the house hand in hand.

"Why don't you start the shower? I'll be up shortly."

"Don't be too long."

I kiss her deeply. "I promise I won't."

After she heads upstairs, I instruct the staff on how I want tonight set up. I plan to take her out on the yacht for a romantic candlelight dinner. After giving instructions to the staff, I quickly send a text to my assistant giving her the approval to proceed with the plans for my office before joining my gorgeous naked fiancée in the shower.

~ * ~

CARI

I'm sitting on the bed wrapped in my robe admiring my stunning rock. I can hardly believe I am engaged to Deven Blake. How I wish Grams and Gramps were alive so I could share this with them.

"If it's not large enough you can pick out something larger."

I look up at him. *Not large enough?* "Oh, this is just perfect."

"Perfect ring for the one perfect lady in my life."

"I'm not per-" He dips his head and kisses me. Mmmm.

"Yes, you are. Now go share our good news."

He reaches for my phone on the nightstand and hands it to me. I dial Rodrigo's number and hold the phone up to my ear while Deven settles down next to me wrapping an arm around my waist.

"Hello sweetie."

"Hello Rodrigo."

"Are you loving your vacation so far?"

"I am! It's been absolutely blissful. Everything couldn't be more perfect."

"Do you expect any less from your billionaire boyfriend? He'll do anything to make you happy."

Well, just about anything. "Yes, he will."

"So if you're enjoying your vacation why are you calling me?"

"There's something I want to share with you."

"What is it sweetie?"

"Deven asked me to marry him last night."

"Well, it's about time. Did you say yes?"

"I did."

"Congratulations! I'm so happy for you. Hunter! They're engaged!"

Hunter gets on the phone. "Congratulations sweetheart! We're so glad it happened sooner rather than later."

Sooner? "Did you know he was going to propose to me?"

"We knew he had a ring for you. We just didn't know when he was going to ask you, but we're glad he finally did. And we're very happy for the two of you."

"Thanks."

"I'll give you back to Rodrigo. Love you C."

"Love you H."

I hear the phone being swapped.

"How big is the bling?"

"It's huge, and quite ostentatious."

"You have to send us a picture of it like right this second."

"I will after we get off the phone."

"Time to tell all. I want to know everything. How did he propose?"

I fill Rodrigo in on the romantic evening Deven had planned from the candlelit dinner to the candlelit beach. It was such a magical moment and something I will never forget for as long as I am alive.

After I get off the phone with Rodrigo, Deven calls his mom. We each take turns speaking to her. Leigh is extremely joyful over the news and lets me know she already considered me to be part of the family from the first time Deven brought me home to meet her.

May is ecstatic when Deven informs her about our engagement, and puts her on speakerphone after she tells him she wants to speak to me.

"Cari!!!!! We're finally going to be sisters! I'm so happy for you and Deven."

"Thanks May."

"What does the ring look like? Did my brother do a good job picking it out? I'm sure he got you a big rock. He only wants the best for you, you know."

Deven rolls his eyes while I'm shocked at how May said all of that in one breath.

"The ring is stunning, and huge. I'll send you a picture."

"You better! I can't wait to be one of your bridesmaids!"

Deven shakes his head. "May, you should ask first. Cari might have already picked out her bridesmaids."

"She has not."

Deven lets out a laugh.

"Your brother is only joking with you. Of course you're going to be one of my bridesmaids."

She lets out a squeal. "Thank you Cari!"

"May, we have to go now. We'll see you when we get back."

"Alright then. Love you both!"

"Love you too sis." Deven ends the call. "She's so bossy."

"I don't think she is. I think she's quite excited about our engagement. She just wants to be a part of our wedding."

He rolls his eyes. "As if we would exclude her. I have to call Brad and tell him the good news."

"While you do that, I'm going to take a picture of the ring and send it to Rodrigo, and May."

Deven shakes his head as he flashes me his dimpled smile that makes my knees weak.

CHAPTER TWENTY-EIGHT

CARI

Halloween has always been one of my favorite holidays, and the charity gala we are going to tonight requires all attendees to come in costumes. I thought it would be ideal for us to go as a famous movie couple. My first choice was Bella and Edward from *Twilight*, but Deven refused hands down. My next choice was to go as Sandy and Danny from *Grease*. He wouldn't allow me to dress up in skin tight leather pants. Finally, I settled on a more conservative couple…Scarlett O'Hara and Rhett Butler from *Gone with the Wind* which got his approval.

Deven accompanied me to the salon early this morning. I wanted to have my hair styled similar to how Scarlett O'Hara wore hers in the movie. He watched as my hair was transformed into a half updo with cascading curls down the back. Throughout the drive home, he seemed transfixed with my appearance staring at me like a lovesick schoolboy.

I managed to hide my costume from Deven. I didn't want him to get a glimpse of it before tonight. It was painstaking to choose just one dress from the selection. I didn't want one of those big puffy gowns and ended up choosing the garnet dress that Scarlett O'Hara wore when she went to Ashley's party. The dress fits me like a glove and has a sweetheart neckline that plunges low. I hope Deven likes how it looks on me. As I am thinking this, there's a knock on the door.

"Can I come in?" Deven asks.

"Yes."

He peeks in and his jaw immediately drops open. He opens the door wider and steps into the master suite. I nibble on my bottom lip waiting for him to comment on my costume.

"Wow Cari! You take my breath away."

"You approve then?"

He pulls me to him, and I can instantly feel his approval. "I very much approve, and will have to fight off all the men who approach you tonight. I'm not letting you leave my side."

"I don't want any of those men. I want only you." I wrap my arms around his neck and bring my lips to his.

"Why don't we forget about tonight and stay home instead?" His fingers reach for my zipper.

"We can't do that. This event is important to you."

He cocks his head, and pouts. "Yeah. I guess we can't."

"You should probably get changed Captain Butler."

He laughs and his eyes crinkle. "How did I let you persuade me to dress up as him?"

"Because I wanted to be Scarlett." Scarlett and I share some common ground. We both lost our mothers, and we both lost a baby. My eyes begin to get misty at the thought of the child we lost and I look away hoping Deven doesn't notice.

"Hey." He gently turns my face back towards him. "What's wrong angel?"

Nothing escapes him. "I was just thinking how perfect everything would be if the baby had survived."

He places a kiss on my forehead. "I promise you that we'll have another baby and give it siblings. We'll have a family. Right now let's just concentrate on us."

He's right. Of course he's right. The doctor did say I will be able to bear children again. I give him a nod.

"Cari, I respect your wish of wanting to keep our engagement a secret for a little longer, but it will make me very happy if I can introduce you as my fiancée tonight."

He's right yet again. I have been trying to prolong him from sharing the news of our engagement, but it will be very difficult to do so tonight. "If it makes you happy then I won't keep you from sharing it."

"It makes me very content. It's about time everyone knows that you're going to be Mrs. Deven Blake."

Mrs. Deven Blake. Hearing him say it brings much joy to my heart.

"I better get dressed in my costume. Care to help me Scarlett?" He wiggles his eyebrows which always earns a giggle from me.

"Why certainly Rhett," I say with a Southern drawl.

Helping Deven change into his costume proved to be a bit more challenging than I thought. Watching him disrobe produced a strong desire in me and we ended up having a quick round of incredible sex resulting in us arriving to the gala a half hour late.

The ballroom is filled with people in costume. There are several George and Martha Washingtons here tonight along with the Jetsons. I even spotted Sonny and Cher. People immediately flock to Deven as soon as they recognize him. *Jeez.* He greets them and then proudly introduces me as his fiancée.

The night passes by quickly with some dancing, an auction, and introductions to a lot of people. News of our engagement spread fast and people constantly came up to Deven and I to offer us their congratulations. Somehow I manage to survive my first gala.

"We're leaving," Deven whispers in my ear after our dessert plates are cleared away.

"Now?"

He gives me a nod. We say our good byes to everyone around the table, and then to more people as we make our way out of the ballroom.

"Deven Blake?"

We both turn around to see who called him by name. *Holy cow!* I am paralyzed by the sight of a scantily clad Pebbles Flintstone standing in front of us.

"Rochelle?"

What is she doing here?

"The one and only." She smiles at Deven and embraces him. He doesn't return her embrace, and the disappointment is clearly evident on her face. She peels herself off of him and narrows her eyes at me.

"I don't believe I have formally introduced you to my fiancée, Cari." Her eyes double in size from what I'm sure is shock. Surprisingly, I can't help but feel smug about it. I have who she wants. I won the grand prize.

"It's nice to meet you," I say not bothering to extend my hand for a handshake. Something overcomes me and for good measure, I place my left hand on Deven's arm making sure she gets a good look at my ostentatious ring. She stares at the ring with daggers in her eyes. Acting this way does not suit me well, but I will not let it trouble me. She needs to know that he chose me.

She turns to Deven not bothering to congratulate us. "I had no idea you were engaged." There is venom dripping in her voice.

"I am indeed. This beautiful lady agreed to marry me a few weeks ago. Kaitlin knows. I'm surprised she did not share the good news with you."

"No. She didn't."

"She should have. Well, if you'll excuse us, we must get going." He interlaces his fingers with mine and we continue to head out of the ballroom and towards the elevator. He places his arm around my waist and kisses the side of my head as we wait for an elevator to arrive.

"You okay?"

I nod to signal I am. "What is she doing here?"

"Beats me."

"Will we be seeing her at every event we attend?"

He plants a kiss on the top of my head. "I hope not."

I silently hope not either. Regardless of the fact that I am engaged to Deven, I will always consider her a threat to me.

"I like that you showed off your ring to her."

"I don't know what made me do it. It's not something I would do, but I wanted her to know that you chose me and that you are completely off limits."

He smirks. "Angel, I have been off limits from the minute I saw you."

And just like that, he makes me forget all about her and makes me remember why I fell in love with him.

CHAPTER TWENTY-NINE

DEVEN

Cari and I are on the way to the airport. I have to go back to Los Angeles for a few days and this time Cari is accompanying me. On the way to the airport, I make a stop at the office first.

"Why are we stopping here? I thought we were going directly to the airport."

"We have time. There's something I want to show you. It's a surprise."

"Oh no. Not another surprise."

I revel in surprising her and will continue to do so for as long as I am breathing.

"You'll love it. I promise."

We step into the lobby together. Everyone who knows her is delighted to see her, and congratulates her and I (again) on our engagement. I catch all of them trying to get a glimpse of her ring. The ladies are dying to see the size of her rock, but Cari dislikes the attention. I give them my get-back-to-work stare, and they all scamper away. With my hand on the small of her back, I walk her to the elevator.

When Catrina spots Cari, she rushes to her and hugs her. Then she lifts her hand to examine the ring. *Women.*

"Whoa! That's some sparkle! Good job Deven."

"Thank you," Cari and I say in unison. We turn and look at each other. She bites her bottom lip trying to hold back her smile.

"Deven, everything is ready for you."

Cari has a quizzical look on her face.

"Good." I take Cari's hand and lead her towards my office. "Close your eyes."

"What's going on?"

I lean in and kiss her cheek. "Like I said earlier, I have a surprise for you."

She closes her eyes, and I guide her into the office until we are standing in the middle of the room.

"Open your eyes."

She opens her beautiful eyes and takes in our newly renovated office. I had my office transformed to accommodate Cari working beside me. She hasn't given me an answer yet about working here, but this nonsense of her working from home every day while I'm here must come to an end. I can work from home as well if I choose to, but certain days I need to be in the office to check on matters, and attend meetings.

Her office occupies the space where I once had my conference table and chairs. In its place now is a desk, and a sitting area. Her desk is an exact match to mine. I turn to her, hold both of her hands in mine, and look into her eyes.

"This is your new office."

She looks back at me with disbelief. "My new office?"

"Yes. I understand your decision has not yet been made, but I want you here working alongside me." I really do. I love spending every second with her.

"Won't you need your own privacy when you meet with someone in your office?"

Damn, she still needs to be convinced. "*Our* office, and that's why I have executive board rooms. I will utilize those rooms to meet with them instead. What do you think of this?"

"I'm flabbergasted. I don't know what to say."

"Say yes."

She walks around her desk. "Alright Deven. Yes, and thank you. Thank you for doing all of this for me."

I almost forget to breathe. She's accepting my proposition. "Stop thanking me."

"How can I not thank you? You have given me so much."

Not nearly enough.

"There's so much more I want to give you. Fortunately for me, we'll have the rest of our lives for me to do so."

There it is. She gives me that sweet pretty smile of hers that makes my heart skip a beat or two.

"I love you." She throws her arms around my neck and kisses me. Score for me.

"I love you too." I plant a kiss on her forehead. "Come. Now we have to get going to the airport."

~ * ~

Cari is jetlagged from the flight. I order in room service while she rests. I attempt to concentrate on the work I have up on my laptop, but find it impossible to take my eyes off of my sleeping beauty. The vibration coming from my cell phone interrupts my focus. It's Kaitlin. I move into the living room to answer the call.

Things between Kait and I have been progressively getting better. She has been seeing Dr. Hammond on a regular basis, and has finally accepted that her relationship with Cal was anything other than normal. That alone was a huge step. She has also been remorseful for the way she treated Cari. She seems genuinely happy I brought Cari along on this trip and wants a fresh start with her. She invites us to dinner, but I decline her offer. It's too soon for her to speak to Cari. We will meet up with Kait another time.

After speaking with Kait, I look out the window at the jeweled lights of Los Angeles. Everything in my life is as perfect as can be, and I can't wait to marry Cari. We haven't picked a date yet, but I'm so damn eager to set a date. The sooner she is officially mine, the better. A set of arms wrap around my waist and I feel the front of her press against my back.

"I was wondering where you went," she says softly.

I place one of my hands over hers. "Kait called. I took the call out here so I wouldn't wake you."

"Oh. Is everything okay?"

I turn around and tip her chin up so I can look at her beautiful face.

"It's all good. She's eager to see you and make things right." She nods her head. "The way she treated you was unacceptable. She understands that now. You don't have to forgive her for how she was towards you, but I ask that you give her a chance to apologize." Cari has a forgiving heart and will do the right thing.

"Yes, of course. I want for us to get along. She will be my sister-in-law, and I don't want there to be any awkwardness."

I kiss her, and then brush her hair behind her ear. "I want you to understand that you are the most important person in my life. I can survive without Kait, but I cannot survive without you. I tried it once and I barely kept my head above the water."

"We'll never be apart."

"I promise you angel we never will be again."

I rather be dead than to ever let her out of my life again.

CHAPTER THIRTY

November

CARI

Deven and I made plans to meet Rodrigo and Hunter in Chinatown for lunch on this sunny and brisk autumn day. We arrive forty-five minutes ahead of schedule and use the time to wander through the crowded streets of Chinatown. Secretly, I'm grateful that Jordan has been given the day off. Deven was quite hesitant at first to give him the day off as he wants to have a bodyguard with us at all times, but we needed a break from him. Sometimes there is no privacy and it's something I must address with Deven.

During my short residence in Chelsea, Rodrigo and I often went to Chinatown. There are so many restaurants to choose from, and all at very reasonable prices. Deven and I arrive at the restaurant where we agreed to meet them for lunch. It's crowded as usual and we have to squeeze through in order to reach the hostess stand. Deven tells the hostess how many people are in our party and is given a ticket with a number. Once our number is called we will be shown to our table.

"Great timing," Deven says sarcastically. I turn around to see him looking down at his phone. "Got to take this angel. Be back shortly."

I nod and watch him leave the restaurant. I look around and watch the ladies wheeling carts with small dishes called dim sum in it. My phone rings, and I pull it out of the Gucci handbag that Deven purchased for me.

"Hello?"

"Hi sweetie. We'll be there soon. We're running just a tad behind." In Rodrigo's terms, that means they are running ten to fifteen minutes behind.

"You don't need to rush. We are waiting for a table."

"Hopefully a table will be ready when we get there. See you soon."

"See you." I end the call and unexpectedly the hair on the back of my neck stands up. I look back and catch an Asian man staring at me. He makes me feel uncomfortable, and I can't help wishing Deven hurries back. I force myself to look away, but every now and then I turn back around to find him still staring at me. I begin typing a text to Deven asking if he can accelerate his conversation and return. As I am about to hit the send button, the Asian man approaches me.

"Excuse me. I don't mean to sound cliché, but you seem very familiar to me." My eyes widen. He's trying to pick me up!

I search for the right words to say. "That can't be possible."

He slides his hands into his pockets and purses his lips briefly. "I believe it is possible. Are you related to Charlotte Snow?"

A gasp escapes my lips. I am completely taken aback by his question.

"How do you know her?"

"I went to high school with her."

I cannot believe that after all these years I would run into someone who knew my mother. What are the odds of such a thing happening? A million questions swirl in my head like a tornado.

"Were you a friend of hers?"

"You can say that. You look an awful lot like her. Any relations to her?"

"Yes, there is. I'm her daughter, Cari."

"Her daughter?" Now he's the one who seems taken aback.

"Yes, sir. And may I ask who you are?"

"Certainly. My name is Max Lew." He offers a handshake.

I shake his hand. "It's very nice to meet you."

"Hi baby doll. I'm sorry I kept you waiting," Deven says as he slips his arm around my waist. He stares Mr. Lew down with the back-off-or-you-will-be-sorry look. Oh, he can be so possessive.

"Deven, I want you to meet Max Lew. Mr. Lew, this is my boyfriend, Deven."

"Fiancé," Deven corrects me.

"Nice to meet you. And please call me Max."

The two cordially shake hands.

"Newly engaged?" Max asks.

"Yes," I immediately reply.

"My congratulations to you both," Max says.

"How do you know Cari?" Deven asks.

I answer for Max. "Max went to school with my mother."

"Is that so?" Deven asks.

"It is," Max responds.

"It's astonishing you remember what my mother looked like after so many years have passed."

"Your mother was a beautiful young lady, and you resemble her a lot."

Deven pulls me closer to him making me peer up at him. His eyes are narrowed and he has *that look* on his face.

"Did you know her mother well?"

Max shakes his head. "Unfortunately not."

"That's too bad. I'm sure Cari would have enjoyed hearing some stories about her mom during her school years."

The hostess calls our number. I don't want our conversation to end. I want to know what he remembers about my mother.

"Our table is ready. Would you like to join us?" I ask

"I'm sure Max has his own lunch plans," Deven answers.

"Thank you for offering, but I am waiting for my family to arrive."

"Oh, of course. Well, it was very nice to meet you Max," I say.

"It was nice to meet you both."

"Good day Max," Deven says as he holds my hand and we follow the hostess to our table.

Deven pulls out the chair for me first, and then claims the chair on my left side. The waiter places four settings on the table. Each setting consists of a small plate, a Chinese tea cup, and chopsticks. After the waiter leaves, Deven drapes his arm over the back of my chair, and leans into me.

"How did you meet Max?"

"He was staring at me, and I was about to send you a text to come back when he initiated conversation with me."

Deven's eyebrow arches. "About your mother?"

"He asked me if I was related to Charlotte Snow, and I asked him how he knew of her. That's when he told me they went to school together."

"I find it bizarre he would run into you here of all places."

What is he implying? "Deven, are you insinuating that he planned this?"

"Anything is possible." There he goes with his overprotective self.

"It is not possible. It's pure coincidence."

"No." He shakes his head. "I don't believe it."

I touch his cheek. "I love you. Let it go. There was no harm."

"But there could have been. That's why I hired Jordan and was reluctant to give him the day off."

"Nothing happened."

"Nothing happened because I showed up in time. I better not ever see him around you again."

"I don't think you have to worry about that."

"I'm only concerned about you."

He kisses my cheek.

"Awww. Don't you just love when you see people in love Hunter?"

My best friends have arrived. Deven pulls back and we get up to give them a hug.

"I'm starving," Hunter says taking his seat.

"As always," Rodrigo says.

"A rigorous workout makes me hungry."

One of the ladies approaches our table with her cart and Rodrigo asks what she has. She removes the cover off the small plate to show him, and Rodrigo puts up four fingers to indicate he wants four plates of the dim sum. She removes the lids off the plates and squeezes some soy sauce over the food before setting it down on the table.

Hunter picks up his chopsticks right away and starts to eat. Rodrigo rolls his eyes and shakes his head. He knows there is nothing he can do when Hunter is hungry.

"Have you two picked a date for your wedding yet?" Rodrigo asks.

Deven and I turn to each other and smile. We had finally selected a date and location last week. I had wanted to share the good news with Hunter and Rodrigo then; however, Deven preferred that I tell them in person.

"We have," Deven says.

"So when is it?"

"June eleventh," I reply.

Rodrigo sets his chopsticks down on his plate and claps softly. "Perfect! Now the fun begins as to where you will have your ceremony and reception."

"We've chosen where we want to get married."

"You have? Where?"

"In Newport."

"Rhode Island?"

"Yes."

"Will it be at your family's house Deven?"

Deven rubs the back of his neck. "No, it won't be there."

Rodrigo's eyes widen. "Are you getting married in a mansion?"

I give him a nod.

"Oh my God! What a dream come true. I can't wait to help plan the wedding." Rodrigo has a smile from ear to ear.

"We will be hiring a wedding planner," Deven chimes in.

Rodrigo's smile fades. "*What?!* Why do you need to hire a wedding planner when you have me?"

Oh no. I sense a battle coming on over the wedding planner.

"Because I want Cari to have the wedding of her dreams," Deven says.

"So do I. But what does the wedding planner know about Cari? Nothing. And who knows her better than I do? I can plan the wedding of her dreams."

"I don't need a big wedding," I interject.

"Of course you do angel. You should have a big and grand wedding."

"I agree with Deven. You are elevating yourself to a new status. Start it off right."

My heart is in Deven's hands. My life will change once I marry him, but I am ready for it. I can't wait to become his wife.

CHAPTER THIRTY-ONE

CARI

The weeks have flown by, and Thanksgiving is only a week away. Rodrigo and I have always spent Thanksgiving together, but now that he's married to Hunter they will be spending it with his family in California this year. Deven and I plan to go to his mother's house for dinner. As I will be a part of the Blake Family soon, I volunteered to make a side dish and bring it to dinner even though Leigh insisted it is not necessary.

I take a day off to complete my grocery shopping before heading into Manhattan to have lunch with Deven. I wait for him in the lobby of the BG building as he concludes his late running meeting.

"Good afternoon Miss Cari."

"Good afternoon Keith."

Keith is one of the dedicated security agents who have been with the company for many years. He always has a pleasant demeanor.

"Going up to see Mr. Deven?"

"He requested I wait for him here. He should be down shortly."

He nods. "Very well. What are your plans for Thanksgiving?"

"I will be spending it with Deven and his family."

"Ms. Leigh makes a mighty fine meal."

"Yes, she does. And what are your plans?"

"Me and my wife are going to our son and daughter-in-law's in New Haven. My daughter-in-law is due in a couple of weeks."

"Oh, congratulations! Is this your first grandchild?"

"Yes, it is."

As Keith is telling me about how excited he and his wife are about being grandparents, I recognize the Asian man from Chinatown standing in the far corner of the lobby. He waves to me. What is he doing here? I wrap up my conversation with Keith and excuse myself to walk over to him. The gentleman sees me, and a warm smile instantly appears on his face. He's well dressed in a three piece business suit with a wool coat over it.

"Max, right?"

"Yes. How good it is to see you again Cari."

"Um, yes. It's good to see you again as well. Are you waiting for someone?"

He shakes his head. "Actually, I came to see you."

"Me?"

"Yes."

"How did you know to find me here?"

"It's not hard to find information on you through the internet. Plus your fiancé is an easy search."

Something about his confession makes me uneasy. "Is there something I can do for you?"

He lets out a deep breath. "I came here because I have something I want to tell you."

It must be something about my mother. "Why don't we go over to the atrium and sit down to talk?"

"No, that's quite alright. This shouldn't take long."

I am eager to know what it is he has to tell me. "What is this about?"

He crosses his arms. "Your mother." Just like I thought.

"My mother?"

"Yes. I knew your mother."

"You had mentioned that."

"Yes, I did. She was very beautiful."

"You mentioned that as well."

"You look a lot like her."

"You had mentioned that too. And my grandparents used to tell me that all the time."

"Did they ever tell you who your father is? Do you know who he is?"

I shake my head. "No, unfortunately I do not know who he is." Oh my

God. Maybe he knows who my father is.

He purses his lips and then lets out a sigh. "You're looking at him."

What? My jaw drops open from his startling revelation.

No, he can't be. Impossible.

To be continued…

Books by R.C. Stern

Fate + Chance = Love (The Blake Family Series Book 1)
Simple + Complicated = Impossible (The Blake Family Series Book 2)

Stay tuned for the final installment of Cari and Deven's story!

Acknowledgements

First and foremost, the biggest thanks to my readers.

To my brother: *"There's no other love like the love for a brother. There's no other love like the love from a brother." - Terri Guillemets*

To my sons: *"Sons are the anchors of a mother's life." - Sophocles*

To my family: *"Everyone needs a house to live in, but a supportive family is what builds a home." - Anthony Liccione*

To my friends: *"I didn't find my friends; the good Lord gave them to me." - Ralph Waldo Emerson*

To my best friend: you truly are a godsend and more. Thank you so very much for always being there, for listening to me, for giving me advice and feedback, etc. The list continues to grow. I am so fortunate to have you in my life. You are indeed amazing and very special to me. *"Some people arrive and make such a beautiful impact on your life; you can barely remember what life was like without them."- Anne Taylor*

To my two "angels": *"The best kind of friendships are fierce lady friendships where you aggressively believe in each other, defend each other, and think the other deserves the world." - Unknown*

To my musketeers: *"Good friends help you to find important things when you have lost them: your smile, your hope, and your courage." - Doe Zantamata*

To my "DAH": *"A good friend is a connection to life — a tie to the past, a road to the future, the key to sanity in a totally insane world." - Lois Wyse*

Connect with R.C. Stern

Facebook: www.facebook.com/authorrcstern

Goodreads: www.goodreads.com/R_C_Stern

Instagram: authorrcstern

Pinterest: www.pinterest.com/authorrcstern

Twitter: www.twitter.com/author_rcstern

www.ingramcontent.com/pod-product-compliance
Lightning Source LLC
Chambersburg PA
CBHW060231180626
46813CB00007B/3040